THE CALL OF THE ISLES

One memory lingers from Lara Daniels' childhood holiday in Shetland, that of having her hand held by someone loving and strong. Returning years later to work as a GP and to be near her boyfriend, Doctor Tony Adams, she learns the secrets of her past. From her grandfather, a Norwegian who made many runs with the famous 'Shetland Bus' during the war, she hears of her grandparents' ill-fated love affair. But it is local fisherman Magnus Cameron who forces her to question her own feelings.

Books by Shirley Worrall
Published by The House of Ulverscroft:

A NEW FUTURE BECKONING

SHIRLEY WORRALL

THE CALL
OF THE ISLES

Complete and Unabridged

ULVERSCROFT
Leicester

First published in Great Britain in 1995

First Large Print Edition
published 2000

British Library CIP Data

Worrall, Shirley
The call of the isles.—Large print ed.—
Ulverscroft large print series: romance
1. Love stories
2. Large type books
I. Title
823.9'14 [F]

ROM
1465574

ISBN 0–7089–4200–8

Published by
F. A. Thorpe (Publishing)
Anstey, Leicestershire

Set by Words & Graphics Ltd.
Anstey, Leicestershire
Printed and bound in Great Britain by
T. J. International Ltd., Padstow, Cornwall

This book is printed on acid-free paper

1

Lara P. Daniels. The signature flowed from Lara's pen with a confident flourish. She double-checked the application form, then, satisfied, she kissed it for luck.

'I bet it doesn't turn into a prince,' a voice called across the hospital canteen.

Laughing, Lara turned around in her chair. 'You never know what it might turn into Tony.'

'That sounds ominous. Coffee?'

'Please.'

Lara watched Dr Tony Adams walk to the counter. He walked stiffly, favouring his right leg more than usual, a sure sign that he'd had a long, tiring day. Betty, behind the counter, said something to make him smile as she poured the coffees and, for a moment, the smile hid the signs of weariness in his face. Unfortunately, the moment was brief. Given the long hours he'd been working lately, Lara supposed it wasn't surprising he was tired.

She couldn't help remembering the way he'd been when she first met him, when he'd been blessed with seemingly endless energy and enthusiasm. Like many of the female staff at the hospital, Lara had promptly fallen in love with his good looks. Tall, with wavy, sand-coloured hair and warm brown eyes, Doctor Adams had caused many a heart to flutter.

He and Lara became firm friends from the start. In fact, Lara had allowed herself to dream a little, until Tony began dating Jane Clarke.

Lara and Jane didn't get to know each other well. They'd been so totally different that there had been no easy starting point for a friendship. Even in appearance, they couldn't have been more different. Jane was as dark as Lara was fair. She was short and bubbly, whereas Lara was tall and more serious.

Within six months of their first meeting, Jane and Tony were married . . . And far too short a time later, Jane had been killed.

Tony carried two coffees and an assortment of sandwiches over to her table and sank thankfully into the chair opposite.

'You look tired,' she said. 'Bad day?'

He gave her a wry smile. 'I'm still recovering from last night.'

'It was your suggestion that they join us,' Lara pointed out with a laugh.

After the usual day fraught with problems, they'd decided to try a restaurant that had recently opened nearby. They'd wanted nothing more than good, simple food, in a relaxing atmosphere.

They'd been at their table for less than fifteen minutes when two newly-married friends, Nick and Carol, arrived. After a meal that was long and drawn-out, although highly enjoyable, Tony and Lara were persuaded to visit their new home. They even had to make a torchlit inspection of the garden they were so proud of. By the time Tony had finally driven her home, Lara had been asleep on her feet.

'How's your day been?' he asked now.

'Chaotic! I fielded that RTA on the motorway. We were lucky, it was mostly cuts and bruises. It's just as well, because we don't have a single spare bed.'

Tony nodded at the application form that she'd half-hidden. 'Why the kiss?'

Lara hesitated. She'd wanted to give him the good news when they were alone, not when they were grabbing a quick break amid the constant to-ings and fro-ings of the hospital. But her excitement got the better of her.

'I was saving it for a surprise but — ' She handed him the application form.

'I might not even get considered,' she warned as she watched him read. She waited for a huge, beaming smile to light his face but instead, she saw his eyebrows draw ever closer together in a frown.

'Whither thou goest, I will go?' He glanced up. 'What is this, Lara? It's three months since I first applied for my new job — eight weeks since we knew I'd got it. Never once have you mentioned you might want to work in Shetland, too.'

Lara had expected him to be surprised, yes, but she'd thought his pleasure would far outweigh any other considerations. 'I thought you might be pleased. Well — I hoped you would!' Tears were dangerously close, but she refused to give way to them.

'Pleased? That we'd be ten miles apart instead of nearly eight hundred?' he teased. 'Look at me, Lara. Come on — look at me!'

She glared across at him, and he chuckled.

'You don't have to be so fierce about it. I'm not pleased — I'm delighted!'

Lara felt a rush of relief. They'd reached a delicate stage in this relationship. She knew neither was ready to make a final commitment but, for a moment, she thought she'd blown it.

To Lara, the vacancy in Shetland was a gift. It was as if Fate or Lady Luck had conjured it up especially for her.

Tony sat back, cupping his mug in his long

fingers. 'So what brought this on? Looking for your roots? Or — ' his voice deepened ' — Did you just think you'd miss me too much?'

She laughed shakily.

'A bit of both, I suppose.' She paused, trying to get her thoughts together. 'When we were talking, just after you'd got the job, about all it would mean — how much you were looking forward to the slower pace, and getting to know the people you were treating . . .'

'Mmm. That's the bit I'm looking forward to.' He sipped his coffee. 'I've never spoken to you about this, Lara, but we both know another reason I'm moving so far away.'

Lara nodded and briefly touched his hand. 'Jane.'

Lara knew, perhaps better than anyone, what Tony had been through. She also knew that he had to come to terms with a lot of things before he was ready to make a fresh start with someone else. First and foremost, he had to stop blaming himself for Jane's death.

Theirs had been a stormy marriage from the start. Jane, the only child of doting parents, had been spoilt all her life and Tony, blind to her faults, had been happy to continue spoiling her. It hadn't been enough

5

for Jane, though. She'd resented his work, and the long hours it entailed. She loved her amateur dramatics, and was very talented, but she had always wanted more. She resented Tony's absence and perversely, when they went out in company, she would spend her time in vivacious chat and laughter with Tony's male friends.

One day, it had all proved too much, even for Tony.

Lara could remember the day as if it were yesterday.

One of Tony's patients had died and the fact that it had been a high possibility hadn't made the loss any easier. He'd gone home to Jane needing her understanding, but it hadn't been forthcoming. Tony, in no mood for her demands, had provoked what soon became a blazing row.

Jane had stormed out of their house, with Tony close behind. In a blind rage, she'd dashed into the road, straight into the path of a car. Tony had tried to pull her back.

He had escaped, badly injured but alive. Jane had been killed instantly. The driver hadn't stopped and had never been traced.

Now, over two years later, the physical scars that Tony bore were few. Apart from a limp that was only noticeable when he was tired, he'd made a complete recovery.

Mentally, too, he was almost back to his old self. Lara just wished he could find a way to forgive himself.

At first, he'd buried himself in his work, but then he and Lara had started going out to the cinema, to dinner together, or to the occasional concert.

Lara had been under no illusions. He'd chosen to take her out because he'd known that, with Lara, he didn't have to pretend. Nowadays it was different. They enjoyed being together.

Even so, she knew he wasn't ready to commit himself to anything permanent, just as she wasn't ready to tie herself to a man who still blamed himself for his wife's death.

'You know how long I've been wanting to get into general practice.' Lara broke the silence. 'And unless a miracle happens, this place will have closed in twelve months' time.'

'Oh, it's a good time to move. Thought so myself!' He smiled at her.

'And I've always been curious about Shetland. Who knows, if Mum had married a local boy, I might have been living there now.'

'And married to a local boy yourself?' Tony's voice was teasing.

Before Lara could respond, his pager bleeped. With a groan, he took a swallow of rapidly cooling coffee and went to the wall phone.

Lara watched him speaking. He seemed amused at first.

I hope I get this job, Lara thought. I don't want this to fizzle out just because we aren't in the same town any more . . .

Tony laughed briefly, said something else, replaced the receiver and returned to their table, grinning.

'That,' he told her, 'was Doctor Burrows.'

Laughter bubbled up. 'I don't think he's been home all week,' Lara said. 'Mind you, when the novelty of having qualified wears off, he's going to be a very good doctor.'

'When,' Tony agreed with a smile. 'I suppose we were all equally unbearable. I remember hoping and praying that I'd hear those magic words 'Is there a doctor in the house?' I was poised to leap to the rescue and save lives. Of course, it never happened.'

He sat down and took her hands in his. 'I can't believe you're doing this, you know. You're sure it's what you want? You're applying for — well — the right reasons?'

'Yes.' Lara was confident about that, and it showed in her voice. 'Junior partner in an island practice. It sounds right for me. It's the sort of challenge I want. Honestly!'

He squeezed her hands in his. 'Well, for

purely selfish reasons, I'm delighted.'

'I haven't even got an interview yet,' Lara reminded him.

'A lady of your talents? You'll walk it!'

★ ★ ★

When Lara got home that evening, her first impulse was to tell her parents the news. But she recognised the car parked outside. Hazel Palmer, one of her mother's friends, would be holding forth. She let herself into her flat at the back of the house.

Hazel's main topic of conversation at the moment was her grandchildren and, after one of her visits, Lara's mother was unable to resist reminding Lara that she hoped one day to have grandchildren of her own.

Given the number of cousins she had, Lara had never considered herself an only child but, at times like this, she wished she had brothers and sisters to provide the much-wanted grandchildren.

At least today she had some news which would steer the conversation away from her husbandless, childless state. Her parents, her mother especially, would be delighted.

And yet . . . it had struck Lara as odd how, telling them about Tony's imminent move to Shetland, the news had been greeted with shocked surprise. The change was just what Tony needed and she'd expected them to be happy for him. Instead, there had been a distinct lack of enthusiasm.

Only afterwards had it occurred to her that they were probably hoping to hear wedding bells, and Tony's departure had made those a little less likely.

At first, they'd worried about her getting involved with a man who had lost his wife in such tragic circumstances but once they'd got to know Tony, and grown to admire him, their feelings had changed considerably.

As soon as she told them she was hoping to follow him to Shetland, her mother would be planning the colour of her wedding outfit.

Lara smiled at the thought, and then reminded herself again that she hadn't got the job yet. Convincing herself that Lady Luck had conjured up that job especially for her was fanciful nonsense, and she knew it. There could be dozens of more suitable applicants.

Not that she wasn't suitable but she didn't know what sort of person they were looking for. If the other doctor in the practice was a woman, for instance, it was likely — not that they'd ever admit to such a thing — that they would want a man. If the other doctor was young, they might want someone older . . .

The health authority had to consider the

patients' wants and while some liked to see women doctors, some preferred men. And while Lara hated the word discrimination, she knew that such matters entered the equation . . .

By the time she'd showered, cooked herself an omelette and eaten it, Hazel's car had gone. Lara grabbed her key, left her flat and let herself into her parents' home.

'It's only me,' she called out.

Her mother was on the phone, so Lara went into the living-room and found her father catching up with the day's news.

Lara kissed him, folded his newspaper for him and put it down on the table. 'How's Hazel?'

He chuckled. 'You don't want to know.'

'Not another grandchild?' Lara asked warily.

'Not quite — just another on the way. Judy and Peter. And Judy.' he added teasingly, 'is two years *younger* than you, Lara.'

Lara was forced to laugh as he repeated one of her mother's stock phrases. She knew her father was equally keen to see her settled with a family, but he never pushed the issue. For that, Lara was grateful.

'You'd feel old if I made you a grandfather,' she replied lightly.

'Rubbish!'

It was, too. For a man who spent the largest part of his day sitting behind his desk in the London offices of an international oil company, Robert Daniels was in surprisingly good shape. He was a large, broad-shouldered man with thick, dark hair and grey-blue eyes. Lara had inherited those eyes, but her fair colouring and fine, blonde hair had come from her mother.

Margaret Daniels, a woman who was as energetic as her husband, came into the room. 'Lara, what a lovely surprise. I've just been talking about you. Hazel was here, and you'll never guess — '

'I will, Mum,' Lara said quickly. 'Judy's expecting a baby, which is wonderful news. But actually, I've got some news myself.'

Her mother's face lit up. 'Tony's changed his mind about leaving?'

Lara laughed. 'Of course he hasn't. No, I've applied for another job — in general practice.'

'Now, that is good news,' her father said immediately. 'It's no use waiting until the hospital closes.'

'Where is it?' her mother asked.

'That's the best part,' Lara told them happily. 'It's in Shetland as well. Of course, there's no guarantee that I'll get it — '

'Shetland?' her mother said flatly.

12

'Yes, but she'll be near Tony.' Lara's father moved closer to her and touched her arm. 'Isn't that the way of it, Lara?'

'Is that it?' Margaret asked.

'Not altogether, Mum. It sounds a great job. And with Tony going — well, when I saw this advertised, I thought it was perfect.'

'I told you, Rob.' Margaret turned to her husband. 'I told you something like this would happen.'

Lara was horrified to see tears glistening in her mother's eyes.

'If you're only going because of Tony — ' Margaret began.

'I'm not.' Lara was puzzled. 'I'm going for a whole host of reasons.'

'Such as?' Robert demanded. 'From London to Shetland — talk about extreme. How do you know you'll like it? Wouldn't it have made more sense to have at least had a holiday there?'

'Come off it, Dad,' Lara scoffed. 'I could have applied for a job in Birmingham, Cardiff or anywhere. I wouldn't take a holiday just to make sure I liked the scenery. A job's a job!'

'Couldn't you at least have talked it over with us?' Margaret asked.

'I *am* talking it over with you. This is the first chance I've had.'

Lara looked from one to the other.

Whatever she'd expected, it wasn't this. Her father looked as if he couldn't believe it, or didn't want to believe it, and her mother . . .

'What's the problem?' Lara asked in amazement. 'I know it seems a long way away but it's only four hours by plane. It's where you were born and brought up, Mum. Naturally it would be nice for me to work in a place you know so well. It's a lovely place, too, by all accounts.'

A terrible thought struck her. 'Oh no! Mum, you're not ill, are you?'

'No, no,' her father said quickly. 'No, it's not that.'

'I don't think you'll be happy there,' Margaret burst out. 'I wasn't — until I met your dad — and I don't think you will be.'

'Mum,' Lara said carefully. 'It was your parents you didn't get on with. It had nothing to do with the place.'

'Yes, it had. It was my parents, the place — everyone knowing everything about everyone else up there. Everyone thinking — ' Her voice wavered.

'It's a tight-knit community.' Lara agreed, completely bewildered, 'but isn't that part of its appeal? Isn't the worst thing about London the fact that many people don't even know their next-door neighbour?'

'I hated it,' Margaret said fiercely.

'Your mother had a very unhappy childhood,' Robert said, offering an explanation that was no explanation at all.

'We never told you,' Margaret said, clearly trying to pull herself together as she dabbed her eyes with a handkerchief. 'We should have, I suppose, but it never seemed important. As a family, we had as little as possible to do with — with my parents. My family was here. It still is, Lara.'

'Told me what?' Lara asked with a frown.

'About — my parents,' Margaret said in a tight whisper. Her husband took her into his arms, and Lara watched, aghast at the depth of feeling between them.

'Mum, what is it? I had no idea!'

'Come on, Margaret, let's all sit down.' Robert Daniels coaxed, but she shrugged him off, walked over to the window and stared out into the darkness.

'Iain Sutherland, my father — God, that's a laugh — was a very bitter man, prone to bouts of terrible anger. He had reasons, I suppose. He'd gone off to war strong and healthy, full of ideals; he came back crippled for life.'

Her back was straight and tense. She swallowed before she went on.

'My mother was totally different. She was everything I longed to be — lively, laughing,

15

patient with Iain and his rages.'

She turned round to face Lara.

'I was twelve when I learnt that, during the war, when her husband was away fighting for his country, she met a Norwegian. That Norwegian, that Anders Larsen, was my father. He — '

'Margaret,' Robert broke in gently, 'don't upset yourself.'

Margaret carried on as if she hadn't heard him.

'You're right, Lara. It is a tight-knit community. I lived with that, always wondering if people knew, or if they simply suspected.

'Never knowing who might be looking after me as I walked along the road . . . ' She shuddered. 'I loathed it.'

Lara was appalled.

'Oh, Mum — how did you find out?'

'Someone told Iain.'

The reply was too quick, too offhand. What isn't she telling me? Lara thought.

'Iain and my mother had the most terrible row.' Margaret added. 'and I heard every bitter, furious word of it.' The tears filling her eyes couldn't be held back any longer. Margaret gulped, said, 'I'm sorry,' and ran from the room.

Neither Lara nor Robert made any attempt

16

to stop her. Lara flopped back in her chair. A host of questions raced through her mind but she was too shocked to voice any of them.

Her father paced the length of the room, clearly worried, until Lara broke the silence. 'I had no idea. Why was I never told?'

'There never seemed any point,' Robert admitted, a little ruefully. 'It just didn't come up. The last time you saw your grandparents you'd have been — I don't know, four or five, I suppose. You were too young to understand then and — well, it's never seemed important.'

Lara grimaced at that. It seemed important now.

'We spent a fortnight in Shetland with them before you were at school.'

'I don't remember that.'

Yet, when she and Tony had first discussed his move, she'd pictured it all so clearly. Perhaps something had lingered in her memory after all.

She had only a vague picture of her grandmother, and that was perhaps based on a childhood idea of what a grandmother should be like rather than fact. There were no photos of Moira or Iain in the house, she realised, whereas her father's enormous extended family was framed on every surface.

'It was a disaster,' Robert informed her

dryly. 'Iain was in a lot of pain and he was difficult, to say the least. You were scared of him, love, I remember.

'But it wasn't just him. After that, we decided a clean break was best for all concerned.'

Try as she might, Lara still couldn't understand.

'But it's so unlike Mum,' she said at last. 'Surely in this day and age — I mean, who cares?'

'Yes, Lara, but times were different then. People *did* care. And you know how cruel children can be. Emotions ran high during the war and I'm sure there are many people in your mother's position. The thing was, it was never spoken of.'

'But it's so long ago,' Lara insisted, and her father sighed.

'When I met your mother — '

'I know,' Lara cut in with a smile. 'She'd just accepted a job in Aberdeen and gave it up so that she could marry you. You swept her right off her feet!'

Lara had heard many times of her father's business trip to Shetland, a trip that had ended with him bringing back his bride.

'Something like that.' He chuckled. 'But the thing was, she really couldn't wait to get away. You know her, Lara. She's naturally outgoing, never happier than when she's surrounded by her friends.'

Lara nodded.

'She had very few friends in Shetland. How could she have, when she thought people were sniggering about her behind her back?'

Lara came over to him.

'Oh, Dad, what a mess.'

'I suppose your mind's made up?' he asked.

'It's such a perfect opportunity,' Lara drew back to look at him. 'If they offer it to me, I can't turn it down just because my parents don't want me to go. And why don't they want me to go? Because, half a century ago, my grandmother had an affair with a Norwegian?'

'Put like that, it sounds silly, I know.'

'It does,' Lara said. 'Not my grandmother and this — what was his name? — Anders Larsen? But Mum's attitude to it all.'

'I expect she'll get used to your being away up there.' But Robert clearly hoped she wouldn't have to.

'And fancy not telling me that I've got Norwegian blood running in my veins!' Lara said in amazement. 'A quarter Shetland blood, a quarter Norwegian — what a mixed bag I am!'

Her father smiled.

'I remember a certain eight-year-old telling

every single person she met that she had A
Rhesus *positive* blood in her veins.'

'I remember that, too.' Lara grinned. 'It
sounded so grand that I thought I was
unique.'

'From that moment on, you were deter-
mined to be a doctor.' Robert's frown lines
smoothed out a little, and his smile creases
deepened. 'So, tell me about this job?'

Lara told him, relieved that at last he was
showing some interest. But she was dismayed.
A chance that had seemed almost too good to
be true was now making her feel as if she
were treading around a minefield.

Robert looked up. The stairs were creaking,
and seconds later, Margaret came into the
room, with a tight smile in place, and red eyes
that said, 'Leave it.'

'Lara,' she began, 'you haven't forgotten
Granny Daniels' birthday? The fourteenth of
next month.'

'No, of course not,' Lara said. Had the
whole Shetland issue been pushed aside? 'I've
made sure I won't be working.'

'There should be — ' Margaret paused to
count. 'Twelve grandchildren and seven
great-grandchildren there!'

* * *

20

When the fourteenth rolled round, the seven great-grandchildren were present and correct, but only eleven grandchildren were there; one was working in Edinburgh. Nevertheless, Robert's mother's house was full.

As Lara took her turn with her camera, it struck her afresh that with such a large family on her father's side, it was small wonder that she'd spared little thought for her maternal grandparents over the years.

'I hope you've got my best side, Lara!'

Lara laughed at the seventy-five-year-old whose great-grandchildren were using her as a climbing frame. 'Stop fishing for compliments, Gran!'

Seeing the mob all together — her father's parents, his three sisters and brothers with their partners and children — Lara realised just how much she would miss them all. Apart from enormous gatherings like this one to celebrate her grandmother's birthday, and similar ones over the Christmas period, the year was usually busy with engagements, weddings and christenings.

As a child, Lara had spent her holidays with her parents, an aunt or uncle or two and her cousins. Then, as they'd grown older, she and her favourite cousin, Fran, had explored Spain, Portugal and then Greece together.

Later, when everyone was out in the

21

garden, Lara made the mistake of going inside for a cold drink. There were plates, cups and glasses everywhere. She was loading up a tray to take into the kitchen when Fran joined her.

'Just in time to do some washing-up.' Lara grinned. 'And guess what!'

'Someone's bought Gran a dishwasher for her birthday?' Fran suggested hopefully.

'And what would Gran do with one of those new-fangled contraptions? No, I've got a new job!'

'Lara! That's wonderful. When did you hear? Oh, but I shall miss you. When do you leave? Hey, I bet Tony's pleased.'

Lara smiled at the barrage of questions.

'I heard yesterday, I shall miss you, too, I leave in six weeks and yes, Tony's pleased. He sent me flowers.'

The roses had arrived only a few hours after she'd telephoned him with the news. The card had said, 'The champagne's on ice'.

'And I thought the interview went badly,' Fran scoffed

'So did I,' Lara replied truthfully.

The day had been a nightmare. The plane to Aberdeen had been delayed and, although she hadn't been late for her interview, she'd had no time to collect her thoughts.

On top of that, she'd been too desperate to

convince the panel that she was ideal for the job. She was sure she'd sounded belligerent, pushy, and full of her own importance.

She'd left Aberdeen confident that she'd thrown it all away.

'You realise Aunt Margaret will be hearing wedding bells?' Fran grinned.

Lara only wished that were the case. 'If only that were all.'

'Something wrong?' Fran asked with a frown.

'Mum!'

Lara always confided in Fran, and she needed to talk to someone about her mother's attitude.

'How odd, Lara!' Fran stopped with her hands in soap bubbles. 'And they'd never bothered to tell you? Will your mum be OK once you're there, do you think?'

'She's putting a brave face on it, but she's far from happy about it. Don't ask me why, because I don't know. Dad says it brings it all back to her but that's not like Mum at all . . .

'Tony agrees,' she went on. 'He's convinced there's more to it.' She smiled ruefully. 'He also believes it's none of my business.'

'Illegitimacy was quite a thing in those days,' Fran pointed out. 'It's all well and good being broad-minded when it happens to other people, but perhaps it's different when it happens to you.'

'Perhaps,' Lara agreed doubtfully.

'What about this Norwegian? Anders — your granddad. What happened to him?'

'I assume he went back to Norway after the war.' Lara stacked saucers as she spoke. 'I don't suppose he even knew he had a daughter.'

'It sounds very romantic,' Fran said dreamily. 'The pretty young lass from the islands, the airman fighting for king and country, the dashing Norwegian . . .'

'It was probably nothing of the sort — just another war-time fling with embarrassing consequences. I, for one, wish it had never happened. With Mum as she is, I feel guilty about going.'

'That's ridiculous!'

'I know, but it's true. Mum really is upset about it all. Oh, she congratulated me, wished me luck, had a glass of sherry to toast my future — and yet it was all a show.'

Lara sighed. 'I just wish I could get it over with. Once I'm there, she'll have to accept it. Dad's not much better, either. He knows I'm as stubborn as he is so he hasn't tried too hard to dissuade me. And I think he realises that it's a marvellous opportunity for me. But if it were within his power to stop me going, he'd do it.'

She smiled. 'Sorry. That's enough of my troubles. Tell me how you got on at the auction yesterday.'

Fran ran her own small but rapidly growing business — Shoestring, it was called — interior design on a budget.

'I picked up some lovely pieces.' Fran was fired with her usual enthusiasm. 'I think I can use all of them in those bed-sitters. By the way, did I tell you? The chap who owns them has recommended me to a friend of his who's just bought a couple of holiday cottages in the Cotswolds.'

'That's marvellous.' Lara was delighted. 'I shall use you, too. I want a charming little cottage with a view of the sea. I can already picture it.' Her expression changed. 'You will come and visit me, won't you?'

Fran laughed at her anxiety. 'Try keeping me away!'

'Fran, do you think I'm doing the right thing?'

'Absolutely! If you didn't go, you'd regret it for the rest of your life. Besides,' she added on a practical note, 'if you don't like it, you can always come back.'

★ ★ ★

25

As the plane began its ascent, Lara watched the familiar landmarks of the city disappear from her view. Was her father still watching the plane?

It had been harder than she'd imagined, saying goodbye to her father. They'd arrived far too early and had both been unusually quiet. There had been so many things she'd wanted to say but somehow, they'd all been left unsaid, until her flight had been called.

'I wish Mum — '

'I know,' Robert said gently. 'But she hates goodbyes at the best of times. And this — '

'Isn't the best of times?' Lara finished for him.

'She's been to Shetland twice in the last twenty-five years,' Robert said. 'The first time, for Iain's funeral, I went with her. You stayed with Uncle John, Aunt Sophie and Fran. The second visit was for her mother's funeral, two years ago, and she went alone.'

'I offered to go with her,' Lara pointed out.

'So did I.' Robert nodded. 'But she insisted on going alone. As far as she was concerned, that was her final visit to Shetland. Now she knows different.'

'You'll both come and visit, won't you?'

'Of course we will, darling.' Robert held her close. 'You're not to worry. We're very proud of you. We love you, Lara, you know that. Once your mum's got the first visit over with, you won't be able to get rid of us.'

'You'll keep me posted, won't you?' Lara begged him. 'Tell me how she is?'

'Of course. And don't forget to ring us and let us know you've arrived safely. If there's anything you need — well, we're only a phone call away.'

Passengers were called again and, with tears in her eyes, Lara hugged him tight. 'I'm going to miss you both terribly.'

'Nonsense,' her father retorted, his eyes equally moist. 'You'll be too busy reorganising the health service up there.'

He kissed her and with a gruff, 'Good luck, darling,' he let her go . . .

Changing planes at Aberdeen, Lara was too unsettled to do more than buy a newspaper. She was glad when the smaller plane took off for the final leg of the journey.

What did the future hold for her? Was she making the biggest mistake of her life? Would she make friends and be happy, or would she feel lonely and cut off in a land that boasted a sheep population of three hundred thousand and a human population of a mere twenty-four thousand?

She wondered, too, about Anders Larsen. She would like to know if he ever knew that

Moira had had his child. And would he have cared?

What about Moira? How had she felt, living with that lie for so long?

Was Anders still alive, even? For all Lara knew, he might have been killed during the war. On the other hand, he might be happily living in Norway with a wife, children, grandchildren and great-grandchildren . . .

★ ★ ★

Lara's first sight of Shetland was of a narrow strip of land, flanked on both sides by sparkling blue water. The weather couldn't have been more perfect.

The plane's wheels touched the tarmac, and her eyes filled with sudden tears. Her emotions were so jumbled that she couldn't even begin to understand them.

The first thing Lara noticed when she got off the plane was the fresh, salty air, borne on a gentle southerly breeze.

Sumburgh Airport was small, but it was highly efficient. Within a few minutes, Lara was abandoning her luggage to race straight into Tony's arms. With a laugh, he lifted her off the ground and swung her in the air.

'Welcome to Shetland! I've missed you so much, Lara.'

'Just look at you!' Lara exclaimed, hardly able to believe the transformation. 'You've got a suntan!'

'All this sea air.' He gazed at her eagerly. 'What about you? Good trip?'

'Very good, thanks.'

'No scenes at Heathrow?' he asked gently.

'Mum didn't go.'

'Oh, Lara. I'm sorry.'

'Perhaps it was for the best,' Lara said, shrugging it off. 'Let's get going, Tony. I can't wait to see the place.'

They loaded her luggage into Tony's car and set off on the journey to Lerwick.

'I'll have to get straight back to the hospital, I'm afraid,' he told her. 'But I've booked a table for this evening, if that's OK.'

'Lovely,' Lara replied. 'I'll probably be busy myself. George Rendall, the senior partner, said he'd show me around the surgery.'

She wondered again what Doctor Rendall was like but decided that she'd find out soon enough.

The car sped past heather-covered hills, lochs, green fields, diminutive barrel-shaped ponies, small cottages, narrow country roads leading to places that begged to be explored.

'Lerwick,' Tony announced unnecessarily, as they reached real streets. 'I'll take you through the town.'

Lara was fascinated by the street names. Saint Olaf Street, King Haakon Street, Saint Magnus Street — the place echoed with history.

In the harbour, fishing boats of all sizes and colours shared the water with ferries, yachts, and a bright orange RNLI lifeboat. A gleaming cruise liner looked a little out of place, Lara thought, but, strangely, the replica of the Viking longship looked quite at home.

When they reached the hotel, the well-used phrase 'service with a smile' came into its own. Lara wondered if she'd been lucky with her hotel or if all Shetlanders smiled so readily.

She also wondered how long it took to get used to the dialect. The girl on the desk had understood her perfectly but grasping her reply was a very different matter. The dialect. an odd mixture of lowland Scots and Norse, with a smattering of English thrown in for good measure, was almost musical. It was easy to listen to, if not so easy to understand.

When Tony left, she unpacked, had a quick lunch, then sat in her room. Her initial delight at being surrounded by such spectacular scenery had worn off, leaving her prey to a whole host of doubts and nerves.

Just after two o'clock her phone rang.

'George Rendall is in to see you,' said the

soft, musical voice of the receptionist.

Lara, with butterflies chasing around her tummy, took a deep breath and prepared to meet her new colleague.

* * *

It was almost two weeks later. Lara had picked up a letter in her mother's neat hand from the mat that morning, and had saved it until the evening, not quite knowing what to expect.

They'd spoken several times on the phone. Although Margaret had sounded her normal, happy self, and seemed delighted at how much Lara was enjoying Shetland, she suspected that other feelings might be revealed in her mother's letter.

She drove to a beach she'd spotted days ago but hadn't had a chance to visit, and parked her car. With the envelope in her pocket, she walked down the grassy bank.

A vast expanse of beach, part sand and part shingle, stretched before her. Apart from the gulls swirling above her head, she was completely alone.

As she walked, she thought back over the last two weeks. It had been a busy time, leaving her little time to think.

Her new practice was small, a recent

up-grade having created her own job and one for a nurse. The senior partner, George Rendall, was a kindly, jovial, enthusiastic man in his mid-fifties, who couldn't do enough to help Lara.

She would never forget seeing him in the hotel, his face wreathed in welcoming smiles as he'd said, 'Am I glad to see you!'

He'd taken her to the surgery, then to meet two of his elderly, and Lara suspected, his favourite patients, and then home to meet his wife, Pat.

Pat's welcome had been equally warm. Over a lavish tea — Lara's first high tea — she'd been assured that, when hotel life got her down, she must use the Rendalls' home as her own.

Caroline, the practice nurse, was the same age as Lara, with striking red hair and a laugh that could be heard for miles. Liz, in her forties, dealt with the clerical side and completed a happy team.

Despite its size, the practice was a busy one, but Lara spent plenty of time with each patient, getting to know as much about them as she could. Most people, she knew, disliked seeing a new doctor but the patients she saw gave no indication of this.

How George had managed, being on call twenty-four hours a day and having to arrange a locum before he could contemplate a break, Lara couldn't imagine. No wonder he'd been pleased to see her.

It was Liz Grant who had helped Lara move out of the hotel. Little Bay, a recently renovated stone cottage close to the shore, belonged to Liz's aunt. She was intending to let the cottage to holiday-makers, but was more than happy to accommodate Lara until she could find something to buy.

Lara had moved in the day before, and spent most of the night awake. The very pretty, but thin, curtains let the light in, and she still hadn't got used to the fact that, in the middle of June, it didn't get dark so far north.

She walked to the water's edge, chose a large, flat rock and sat down to read her mother's letter.

She scanned it quickly and then, when she reached the end, read more slowly.

'I'm glad you've settled in so well,' Margaret wrote. 'Your dad sends his love, of course, and needless to say, we both miss you dreadfully.'

She tried to guess her mother's mood. She sounded cheerful, and as busy as ever, but Lara was disappointed. She didn't know what she'd expected exactly, only that she'd expected more.

She'd expected her mother to say how silly she'd been to over-react, and she'd also expected some sort of an explanation . . .

Lara returned the letter to its envelope, put it back in her pocket, and walked on, curious to see what lay on the other side of the cliffs that completed the curve of the bay.

The sun was shining, but a cold wind came across the water, making her pull her jacket closer. The gulls continued to cry out above her as the waves lapped the shore with rhythmic whispers.

When she reached the cliffs, she saw that another smaller bay had been hidden from view.

A sudden shiver ran down her spine. The beach was deserted, but she turned suddenly, feeling that she wasn't alone.

A half-forgotten dream perhaps? No, it was too real for that. She'd been here before, she was sure of it.

Someone had been standing by her side, someone tall and strong. Her small hand had been clasped in a huge, strong hand, and her arm had been raised, reaching up to that hand . . .

Lara walked on, but she couldn't ignore the

power of that brief memory. A strong feeling had enveloped her now. She didn't just remember holding a hand. There had been a feeling of love, a feeling of being safe, and a feeling of complete trust . . .

2

Lara arrived at the surgery early on Monday, ready to wade through an ever-growing mountain of paperwork before she saw her first patient. As soon as she walked into the building, she heard Liz's soft laughter.

'Ah, that sounds like one of our doctors now,' she was saying.

Curious, Lara walked into the waiting room.

'Is there any chance of you seeing an early patient?' Liz asked.

'Of course.'

He was a tall, dark man, in his mid-thirties, Lara guessed, with an obviously painful wrist that he was holding very carefully against his chest.

He'd been smiling when she'd walked in. and, although he was still smiling, he was also looking at her very curiously. Lara wondered if he'd been expecting — or hoping — to see George.

'It can easily wait until nine,' he said.

'And he's spent the last ten minutes telling me he's in agony!' Liz declared. 'That's men for you,' she added with a chuckle. 'A common cold and they're at death's door!'

'It's a well known fact,' the man retaliated with a grin, 'that men don't get *common* colds. *Our* colds are laced with pneumonia and a dozen other things.'

'Ha!' Liz scoffed. 'Away with you, Magnus, before the gangrene sets in.'

Lara laughed as she took the card Liz handed her. She never failed to marvel at how easy Liz was with people, and how perfect she was for her job.

Having been used to the busier, more serious atmosphere of the hospital, where patients came as strangers, Lara found it refreshing to be part of what was almost like a family, where everyone knew everyone else.

'Come with me.' Lara smiled at her patient.

Magnus Cameron, she discovered as she quickly scanned his card, was thirty-five years old and blessed with good health.

'I thought surgery started at eight,' he explained apologetically.

Heaven forbid, Lara thought, as she walked into her office.

'No, the morning surgeries start at nine and the evening ones at six. I'm Doctor Daniels, by the way,' she added, 'I've just joined the practice.'

'Yes, Liz told me. You've come from a

London hospital, I hear. You must find it very different.'

'Very . . . And I'm loving every minute of it. I'd been wanting to get into general practice for some time and the hospital, like so many others, was facing closure.' She smiled. 'Sorry, this isn't getting your wrist treated, is it?'

'I trapped it in a steel rope on the boat yesterday.' He held it out for inspection. 'I hoped it would be better this morning.'

Lara inspected the badly swollen wrist.

'You'll need to go to the hospital, I'm afraid,' she said at last. 'Until it's been x-rayed, it's impossible to say for sure what damage has been done. It could be fractured.'

She took a card from her desk.

'You clearly can't drive. Can you get to the hospital? Now?'

'Aye. My brother's in the car park.'

'Good. I'll put it in a sling for you, in case you have a long wait.'

'Thanks.'

He watched with interest as she prepared the sling.

'What made you choose Shetland?'

'My boyfriend has just accepted a job at the hospital here. I didn't want to be stuck in London traffic jams while he was enjoying all this clean, fresh air.'

38

He laughed.

'And I was curious about Shetland,' Lara went on. 'My mother was born here.'

'Oh?'

'Yes. My grandparents are dead now. My grandmother, Moira Sutherland, died just a couple of years ago.'

His shoulder stiffened under her fingers.

'Dear God,' he breathed. 'You must be Lara!'

'Yes,' she said eagerly, her eyes bright with excitement. 'Yes, I'm Lara. How — ?'

Her voice trailed away. His face had paled, and she had a feeling it had nothing whatsoever to do with the pain from his wrist. The smile had gone, too.

There was so much she wanted to ask, but the shock in his eyes kept her silent, and confused.

'You're the image of your grandfather,' he said in amazement, but then he shook his head. 'No, I'm being fanciful. Perhaps I recognised you from the photograph.'

'Photograph?'

'Granny Sutherland — my brother and I always called her that — had a photo of you in a silver frame. You would have been five or six, I suppose. Never was a photo frame more polished. It gleamed.'

Lara didn't know what to say, and the

room was painfully silent for a moment.

'Alisdair — my brother — was born six days before you. She never forgot his birthday, or mine either come to that, but his birthday always had her wondering what you were doing.

'She used to bake us birthday cakes, with candles, icing, and all the trimmings — I don't suppose she ever stopped hoping that, one day, she'd make a cake for you.' He shook his head sadly.

'When my brother was seventeen, and learning to drive, or eighteen and able to vote — there Moira sat with her long out-of-date photograph, wondering.'

Lara's heart was pounding in her ears. She couldn't even look at him.

'You — you must have grown sick of hearing about me,' she said with a false lightness.

There was no hesitation. 'Yes.'

Lara wished the telephone would ring, anything to break the silence.

'I've still got that photograph,' he said at last.

She looked up in amazement.

'Your mother wanted the cottage and its contents sold as quickly as possible,' he explained. 'I bought it. I live there. It was like a second home to me anyway.'

'And you kept the photograph?'

He nodded. 'It didn't seem right to throw away something that had meant so much to her. Your mother didn't even try to clear it out, so I've got a lot of her stuff.

'Perhaps you'd like to look through it and see if there's anything — ' He shrugged, and his eyes were cold. 'But I don't suppose you'd be interested.'

He glanced at the card requesting the x-ray. 'Thank you. I'll away to the hospital before it gets busy.'

He was at the door before Lara found her voice.

'I had no idea. My mother and my grandparents — they never got along, you see. They — my mother thought it best to make a clean break. Best for everyone. I was only five.'

Magnus Cameron looked at her for a long time.

'Aye . . . well, it's too late to worry now.'

The door closed quietly behind him, and Lara sank down in her chair.

She took the top letter from a pile of correspondence and tried to concentrate on the neat print. But all she could see was a woman polishing a silver photo frame . . .

★　★　★

41

The peace of the evening was suddenly shattered by a frantic ringing of bells. Two children came pedalling furiously round the corner of the narrow road on gleaming, multicoloured bicycles.

Laughing as Lara and Tony leapt on to the grass verge, the children shouted out a greeting and continued on their way.

'At least it's good to see them wearing helmets,' Lara said with a breathless laugh. 'Even if we need them more than they do!'

'I really envy the children here,' Tony said. 'They have so much freedom compared to those in the cities.'

'Mmm.' Lara fell to thinking about her mother's childhood. Margaret had probably cycled along these roads, gathered buttercups and daisies, known every inch of the beaches . . .

'Would you like me to visit your parents while I'm away?' Tony asked, as if reading her thoughts. He was going south for a few days; long enough for his family to see how much good the clean, fresh air and the more relaxed lifestyle was doing him.

'Will you have time?'

'Of course. Any messages?'

'Yes. Tell them I have plenty of room for a couple of guests!'

'I will,' Tony promised.

Lara wouldn't expect any great results. It was only three weeks since she'd seen her parents so, even if all things were equal, she wouldn't expect a visit from them yet.

They walked on, and as they rounded the corner, they came upon a graveyard.

'What a beautiful spot!' Lara gasped. 'But how strange. It's in the middle of nowhere.'

Tony pointed. 'The kirk's down there.'

Lara could just see the top of the small, white-painted kirk. 'Let's have a look.'

At Lara's touch, the iron gate opened with a creak that was more than capable of waking the inhabitants. For all that, the grass was neatly mown and each grave looked well cared for. They walked down the wide grass pathway to the wall at the bottom.

'What a lovely spot,' Lara said again.

While Tony wandered off to explore, Lara stood for a while, marvelling at the silence. Even the gulls seemed to respect this hallowed spot.

She felt a rush of gratitude that providence had brought her here. She couldn't even begin to imagine how lonely she'd have been in London, knowing Tony was here.

In some strange way, she felt as if she had come home. She wanted to settle here, she wanted to belong . . .

'Lara!'

Tony's call broke the spell and Lara walked over to where he was standing. She looked down at the headstone and gasped.

The wording was simple, just two names and two dates. Iain James Sutherland and Moira Anne Sutherland . . . her grandparents. Flowers had been placed on the grave — large white chrysanthemums.

Tony put an arm round her shoulders. Lara had a vivid picture in her mind's eye, of a woman baking a birthday cake while a stranger smiled out of a well-polished silver frame . . .

'I wonder who put the flowers here,' she said at last.

Tony shrugged. 'It could have been anyone. They lived here all their lives so they would have had plenty of friends.'

Lara blinked to keep threatening tears at bay. 'I wish I'd brought some.'

'Lara, you didn't even know they were buried here!'

'I could have found out. I could have asked my mother, or Magnus Cameron. I could have made some effort to find out.'

'Anyway, you don't believe in flowers at gravesides, do you? Flowers should be for the living, you tell me.'

That was true but Lara still couldn't rid herself of a sense of shame.

'It's only as you get older,' she said, 'that you realise how much grandchildren mean to a person. I should have made some effort, Tony. It was all well and good when I was five but as I grew up, a letter wouldn't have hurt, would it? Or a card at Christmas.'

'It wouldn't have hurt your mother to make a duty visit every year or so, either.' Tony hugged her. 'We all have relatives that we'd rather not have. As they say, you can choose your friends but not your relatives . . .

'It's too late now,' he said softly. 'It's history, Lara. You have to live for today and forget yesterday.'

'Oh yes?' Her head came up at that. 'And are *you* forgetting yesterday?'

He flinched and she was instantly sorry.

'I'm trying, Lara.'

Lara sighed. She was in no position to criticise. For years, she'd been far too wrapped up in her own life to spare a thought for a woman, hundreds of miles away, who was gazing at an out-of-date photograph . . .

'Hey. Lara — don't cry.'

She buried her face against him and let the tears fall.

'This isn't like you, Lara,' he said gently.

'I wish they were still alive.' Lara finally lifted her wet face. 'If only Moira had lived for another couple of years. Just two more years, Tony.'

'I know, but life's full of if onlys.'

'Magnus Cameron — ' Lara wiped the tears from her face. 'Oh, he didn't say so, but I knew exactly what he thought about how we'd all neglected Moira.'

'What does he know?' Tony reasoned. 'As a friend, he's bound to be biased. And think of the generation gap. He won't have known what Moira thought of your mother's clean break. Only Moira would have known that.'

'I suppose so,' Lara agreed doubtfully. 'But since speaking to him, I feel so ashamed. And whenever I think of Moira, there's a huge emptiness inside me. It hurts, Tony.'

'I can understand that.' Tony gently brushed a tear from her cheek. 'But you can't blame yourself for something that happened when you were a child. It was your mother's decision, and perhaps she had her reasons.'

Lara took one last look at those perfect white chrysanthemums.

'And perhaps not. That's what I feel, now that I'm here. Too late . . .'

* * *

On Thursday afternoon, Lara had returned from a long walk to a cottage that was crying

46

out to see a duster, when someone knocked on her door.

She opened it to find a smiling, plump woman with dark, greying hair standing there, holding a shining green-leafed pot plant.

'You must be Lara.'

'Yes, that's right.' Lara smiled, feeling at a disadvantage.

After a brief nod of satisfaction, the woman introduced herself. 'I'm Shona Cameron, and what you must think of us I can't imagine. Iain and Moira Sutherland's granddaughter, and we've given you no welcome at all. Whatever would Moira say?'

She handed Lara the plant. 'It's not much, just a wee token to welcome you to Shetland. May I call you Lara?'

'Yes. Yes, of course. And thank you,' Lara said in amazement. 'Thank you very much. Please, come in.'

Shona stepped inside the cottage.

'I don't want to keep you from anything,' she remarked, in a lilting voice that said she hadn't strayed far from the islands. 'I had to come straightaway, as soon as I found out who you were. Moira would be so pleased to know you were working here.

'I wondered if you'd like to come to lunch with us on Sunday?'

'Thank you,' Lara replied immediately. 'I'd

like that very much. Where — ?'

'Oh, listen to me. We're at Burnmouth, the white cottage with the tubs outside. If you take the Lerwick road — '

'Yes, I know it.' Lara had seen the name on the gates. 'And thank you. Thank you for the plant, too. I'd been thinking that a house isn't a home without plants. Sit down, Shona. Can I get you a cup of tea?'

'I can't stop,' Shona said with regret. 'I help out at the day centre and I'm on the way there now.'

'How did you know who I was?' Lara asked curiously.

'Ach!' Shona raised her eyes to the heavens. 'It was Alisdair, my son, who told me. He found out from Magnus, that's my eldest. You saw Magnus, he went to the surgery with his arm.'

'Oh yes. How is he?'

'He'll live. A bone *was* broken but they've strapped it up for him. But why it took him so long to tell us it was you —'

'I was at school with your mother.' Shona added. 'She's younger than me, of course, so we weren't best friends or anything. I haven't seen her for years, except at Moira's funeral, and what a day that was. Gales blowing us off our feet and then the heavens opened!'

Lara didn't know what to say. She felt again

48

that ripple of shame. It would be impossible to explain to Shona why Margaret hadn't been back to Shetland, because Lara didn't even understand herself.

Perhaps when she told her mother about this, and Margaret realised that people she knew were welcoming her daughter with open arms, she would get the whole idea of Lara being in Shetland into perspective . . .

'I must get away,' Shona said, turning to the door. 'We'll see you on Sunday.'

'I'll look forward to it,' Lara promised. 'It's lovely to find someone who knew my family. There's so much I'd like to ask you.'

'We'll have a good chat,' Shona promised. 'And don't bother dressing up; it'll only be the three of us. Four with you, of course. You're not a vegetarian, are you? No? Good. So many are these days . . .'

★　★　★

On Sunday morning, Lara was about to telephone her parents and tell her mother that she was on her way to have lunch with one of her old schoolfriends, but Fran rang her first. Suddenly Lara found she had a lot to tell her favourite cousin.

'Guess what happened this week!' Lara quickly told Fran about her meeting with

49

Magnus Cameron and then with Shona. The call went on and on as they caught up on the news and Lara couldn't help wishing that she was about to sit down to lunch with her parents. She wasn't homesick, there was far too much to see and do for that, but she missed her family, all of them.

Tony had suggested they fly to London together but it hadn't been feasible. She'd had to work Friday and Saturday.

Fran was about to ring off when she suddenly exploded with laughter. 'I almost forgot. Why I'm ringing is to tell you that I've got to go to Aberdeen next week.'

'Fran, that's only a short hop from here. Oh, surely you could manage a day or so here?'

'I was thinking of a week,' her cousin said happily, 'if you can put up with me for that long.'

'But that's wonderful! Which plane will you get? I'll meet you — Heavens, look at the time!' Lara cried. 'I'm late for lunch. I'll have to dash, Fran. Get your flight booked and I'll ring you tomorrow night. OK? I can't wait to see you . . . '

She quickly changed into a blouse and skirt, put a comb through her hair, picked up the flowers she'd bought for Shona and set off for Burnmouth.

The cottage, a traditional, stone-built home, was larger than most and at the side, overlooking the voe, was a large conservatory, filled with flowers. The garden, too, was a mass of flowers and Lara wondered if this was Shona's handiwork.

There were two cars in the drive, and Lara parked on the verge, as far off the road as she could.

She got out of the car and was reaching for the flowers when the door opened and a man came out to meet her. It had to be Alisdair Cameron. He was as tall as his brother, and as dark.

'Hello. I'm Alisdair,' he introduced himself. 'And you're Lara. I feel as if I've known you for years. Welcome to Shetland, and welcome to Burnmouth.'

'Thank you.' Lara was touched by this genuine welcome.

Just then Shona came outside, her face wreathed in smiles of welcome.

'I'm sorry I'm late,' Lara said, handing over the flowers. 'I'm afraid I was chatting to my cousin on the phone, and lost all track of the time.'

'You're not the only one that's late.' Shona told her dryly. Turning to Alisdair, she said, 'Drive over there and see if he's on his way, will you, Ally? And tell him we'll no' wait for him!'

She gazed at the flowers. 'They're beautiful, but you shouldn't have bothered, Lara — it's only our usual lunch. Come on, let me put them in water. Will you have a coffee while we wait? And I'm sorry he's not here yet.'

'Don't be.' Lara laughed, as she followed Shona into a large kitchen. 'I don't feel half so bad about being late now that I know your husband isn't here yet.'

'My — ' Shona's face paled. 'Oh no, lassie. My Robbie's been dead over twenty years.'

'Shona!' Lara was horrified. 'I'm sorry, I didn't realise. I just assumed — when you said the four of us, I automatically assumed — '

'That's my fault,' Shona said with a kindly, if somewhat shaky, smile. 'I should have explained. Magnus always comes to lunch on Sundays.'

'I thought — Well, he said he lived in what used to be Moira's cottage. I'm afraid I assumed — Shona, I'm terribly sorry.'

'Don't take on, lass.' Shona busied herself with the coffee. 'It's a natural mistake to make . . . Anyway, I'm lucky. I've got my two lads.

'Mind you,' she added wistfully, 'there's not a day goes by when I don't miss my Robbie. Silly isn't it, after all this time?'

'Not at all,' Lara said. 'He must have been very young.'

'Yes, but the sea has no respect for age. The sea was his life.' Shona gazed at the voe. 'He went into the fishing like his father before him and like his sons after him.'

Lara sat down at the table with her coffee. Shona was obviously far away in the past — she didn't want to disturb her.

'Robbie was my hero,' Shona said softly. 'He was six years older than me. I spent all my childhood years tagging along with him and worshipping every step he took. Right to the day he died, I thought there was nothing he couldn't do.

'He was my husband, the father of my children, my best friend — and I don't care how it sounds — he was my hero. When you lose your hero, life's never quite the same again.'

'I believe you,' Lara said gently.

Shona emerged from her reverie and turned back to her guest. 'What about you? You haven't thought about marriage yet?'

'I've thought about it,' Lara admitted. 'Tony, that's my boyfriend, was married before. His wife died and I don't think he's come to terms with it yet. He's taken a job at the hospital here, Dr Adams.'

'So you've come here together? Lovely! But

you should have brought him today.'

'He's spending four days in London,' Lara explained.

'Well, there's plenty of time for marriage,' Shona decided.

'Mum doesn't think so.' Lara laughed softly. 'At thirty, she thinks I'm a permanent fixture on the shelf.'

'Aye, well.' Shona chuckled. 'I know how she feels. Magnus is thirty-five, and more interested in fish than girls. Then there's Alisdair, thirty, and he's had more girlfriends than I care to remember. Not a thought of marriage between them.'

A car stopped outside.

'Let's hope there's two of them,' Shona said.

Much to Shona's consternation, however. Alisdair was alone.

'No sign of him.'

Shona tutted. 'I saw him after the service this morning and told him not to be late.'

'I saw him after the service, too,' Alisdair replied, deliberately vague. 'He said something about taking the *Shearwater* out.'

Shona's lips compressed into a thin line of disapproval. 'He should have been born with webbed feet, that one.'

'He'll turn up,' Alisdair said, unconcerned. 'We'll have to start without him. He knows fine that the last to the table gets the least food.'

They waited a little longer but then they did just that. The meal was delicious, the beef the most tender that Lara had ever tasted, and she told Shona so.

'We'd all be tender — ' Shona grinned ' — if we'd spent as long in the oven as this has.'

The company was delightful, with Shona and Lara often having to wipe tears of laughter from their eyes. The questions Lara had been longing to ask about Iain and Moira were answered with amusing stories.

'Moira was a good friend when I lost Robbie,' Shona said reminiscently. 'She seemed to know instinctively how I was feeling, and she always managed to give me hope for the future.

'That was the hardest part, wanting to carry on alone. Although I sometimes felt that — Oh, it's not my place to say.'

'Say what?' Alisdair asked, echoing Lara's thoughts.

'Well, I sometimes felt that her marriage wasn't all it should have been,' Shona said. 'But there, that was none of my business.'

'I shouldn't think Iain was anyone's idea of a perfect husband,' Alisdair put in bluntly. 'He scared us stupid.'

'He was in pain,' Shona said, looking uncomfortable. 'I can just remember him when he joined the RAF. A dashing young chap! And Moira was the prettiest girl for miles. Everyone had expected them to marry, and they did.

'But when he came back from the war, he was a changed man.'

'He had an awful temper.' Alisdair shook his head.

'And so would you if you'd been through what he went through,' Shona said sternly.

'At least he came through it. A lot weren't so fortunate.'

Shona glanced at her watch — again. 'I suppose Magnus has forgotten how to use a phone!' Her expression changed. 'I don't suppose — '

'Ach, no,' Alisdair said. 'He's only out in the bay. He could swim back from there.' He winked at Lara before adding, 'We have learnt the basics, you know.'

'And so had — '

Shona stopped mid-sentence, but Lara heard the unspoken words. '*So had your father.*'

Apart from the fact that the absence of Magnus was beginning to worry Shona, Lara was relieved he hadn't turned up. She couldn't forget the way he'd left the surgery,

56

totally dismissive of the way her family had treated Moira — his 'Granny Sutherland'.

'Do you remember the day I took Iain's wheelchair for a spin?' Alisdair was asking his mother.

Shona laughed at the memory. 'The young devil, nine he'd have been, took the wheelchair while Iain was having a nap in the garden. Both Alisdair and the chair ended up in the sea!'

'He went mad,' Alisdair said. 'It was lucky for me he couldn't run.'

'The best of it was, I got the blame,' Shona remembered. 'He told me I shouldn't have had children if I wasn't capable of keeping them under control.'

The three of them were laughing so hard that they didn't hear the vehicle outside. When the door suddenly opened, Lara was quite startled.

'About time too!' Shona's sharp tone didn't conceal her relief at seeing her elder son safe and sound.

'I know, and I'm sorry,' Magnus said. 'I was out testing the engine repairs on the *Shearwater* when — '

'Is she all right?' Alisdair asked.

'Fine.' Magnus nodded. 'But a call came out that three white-sided dolphins had beached.'

'Dolphins?' Shona's expression softened. 'Are they safe now?'

'One died. It looked as if it had been in a fight. Maybe the others had been guiding it to shallow waters . . . Anyway, we got the other two back to deeper water so they should be OK.'

Lara was fascinated. 'How did you get them to deeper water?'

For the first time, he spoke directly to her.

'With great difficulty! We put them on a stretcher, one at a time, put them on the inflatable, and released them in deep water. The problem is they get very distressed and disorientated, and try to head straight back for the shallows. So we had to hang about, point them in the right direction. You need a few folk for that.'

Turning towards Shona, he added hopefully, 'It's hungry work.'

Shona laughed but headed off to the kitchen, calling after her. 'If it tastes like boot leather, you've only yourself to blame.'

'You ought to come out on the *Shearwater* with us,' Alisdair said to Lara. 'You'd enjoy it.'

'I would not!' Lara retorted with a laugh. 'I risked a trip on the longship, the *Dim Riv*. It rocked and swayed, and I hated every second of it.'

'The *Shearwater* is different,' Alisdair

insisted. 'And you get a far better view of the islands from a boat.'

'I'll take your word for that.'

'Leave the poor lassie alone,' Shona said, putting a plate in front of Magnus. 'It's not everyone's heart's desire to go out on the water. We were just saying, Magnus, about the time Alisdair took Iain's wheelchair and ended up in the sea.'

'Aye, and he gave me a right telling off!' Magnus laughed at the memory. 'He was yelling at me, 'the young devil wouldn't do anything if you didn't put him up to it, Magnus Cameron'.'

'Iain was either terrifyingly fierce,' Alisdair said thoughtfully, 'or very quiet. Either way, he could frighten the life out of you. He wore a permanent scowl, with those enormous eyebrows — '

'Alisdair!' Shona scolded. 'It's Lara's grandfather we're discussing.'

'I want to hear the good and the bad,' Lara said truthfully. 'The thing that worries me,' she added with a smile, 'is that Magnus told me I looked like Iain. Now I'm not sure whether the resemblance is due to the permanent scowl or the enormous eyebrows.'

Her words were met with a surprised silence that was broken at last by Alisdair's laughter.

'The next time Magnus is at the surgery, I'd get his eyesight checked. Believe me, Lara, you look nothing like Iain Sutherland.'

Magnus, Lara noticed, was quietly and purposefully eating his meal.

'Nothing at all,' Shona agreed thoughtfully, 'and yet — it's funny, but I thought I spotted a resemblance to someone. It may just be Meg, my dear — your mother. But there, it could have been anyone. We've all got a double, so they say.'

Talk moved on to Fran's forthcoming visit, and the house hunting that Lara was about to embark on.

They sat for another hour and there wasn't a single pause in the conversation.

Lara felt completely at home, as if she'd known these people all her life. Shona and Alisdair would make anyone feel welcome and if Magnus was a little reserved, and he was, she knew that every time he looked at her, he saw a dear old friend's wistful gaze resting on a silver photo frame . . .

For all that, she knew instinctively that if she had a problem, the Camerons, Magnus included, would do all they could to help.

Finally, Lara had to leave.

'I've blocked your car in,' Magnus said, 'but I'll have to go anyway. We've got an early start in the morning.'

Even so, it was another twenty minutes before Lara was standing on the doorstep.

'Take care, Magnus.' Shona's eyes drank in his every feature as if she might not see him again.

Magnus kissed her briefly. 'Don't fret.'

As they walked to their cars, Lara tried to understand what sort of life Shona had. Having lost her husband, it seemed that she now spent her days worrying about her sons.

'What time do you start in the morning?' Lara asked Magnus.

'Five.'

'Good grief. And what time do you finish?'

'We should be back late Wednesday evening.'

'Wednesday!'

Lara had assumed they went out for the day, caught some fish and came back. Three days on a boat! Her stomach churned at the thought of it. She could see now why Shona worried.

He was about to open the door of his Land Rover when Lara stopped him.

'Those things of my grandmother's — well, I am interested, Magnus. If the offer still stands, I'd like to see them some time.'

'Of course.' He glanced back at her. 'I'll put them ready for you. There are hundreds of mementoes she collected over the years,

61

paintings, wedding photos, things like that. Take what you want. I don't have the room so I'll be glad to get rid of it.'

'Oh no!' Lara was horrified. 'That's not what I meant at all!'

Was that what he thought, that she was descending like a greedy vulture? Is that how it had sounded?

'I know it's a bit late but I would like to know a little about my family.' Her face was burning with embarrassment. 'I'd like to see her wedding photos,' she added lightly. 'Who knows, perhaps I'll spot a resemblance between myself and Iain.'

A flush of colour crept into his face. 'Aye, well, I wasn't thinking when I said that.' He paid exaggerated attention to a small spot of rust on the Land Rover. 'I was confusing Iain with someone else. A Norwegian who lives here. You look a bit like him, that's all. Forget I ever said it . . . '

Lara's heart had begun to pound. He could only mean one person. Anders Larsen.

That meant her real grandfather was still alive — and living in Shetland.

3

For the fourth night in a row, sleep evaded Lara.

During the day, with her work and a million other things to occupy her mind, she was fine, but as soon as she climbed into bed, the questions refused to be silenced.

'Forget I ever said it' Magnus had told her. How could she? How could she forget that, in his eyes, she was the image of a Norwegian? It had to be her grandfather — didn't it?

Of course, Lara told herself as she gave her pillow another thump, anyone with half a grain of sense would have asked him. But no. Lara had made a barely coherent remark about feeling a spot of rain and from this they had endured a painfully stilted conversation on the vagaries of the weather. Then they'd made very hasty arrangements for Lara to call on him on Thursday — tomorrow — to look through Moira's possessions.

Lara's embarrassment had stemmed from something disguising itself as logic or common sense which had put an effective clamp on her tongue. Moira and Iain had been well-respected friends of the Camerons.

How could she tell Magnus that his dear Granny Sutherland had enjoyed an affair with a Norwegian?

It was all very well telling herself that such things didn't matter these days, but in a small community such as this, they *did* matter. Iain and Moira had taken their secret to their graves. What right had Lara to take that away from them?

Lara would be glad when Saturday arrived, bringing Fran with it. She instinctively knew that Fran would understand.

She'd talked it over with Tony, as soon as he'd returned from London, but he didn't really understand. He was understanding — without managing to understand at all. But of course, it wasn't Tony's family.

Telling herself that it was all history, with most of the major players dead, Lara eventually fell into a restless sleep.

The following morning left her with no time to think. She saw ear infections, throat infections, torn ligaments and a host of other complaints, and then made four home visits.

After lunch, she got in her car and concentrated on the directions Magnus had given her for Braeside.

She found it easily and stayed in the car for a few moments, waiting for any memories to surface. Yes, it was now Magnus's home but it had been the Sutherlands' for so long. She had surely stayed in this cottage as a child when she visited with her parents.

No memories came. Not like the one that had flooded over her the day she'd strolled along that beach . . . whose had that strong hand been, clasping hers?

She got out of the car. At first sight, the garden looked overgrown but stopping to look, Lara saw that everything was in its place. The tall shrubs provided a very effective break against what was becoming a strong westerly wind.

'It was tidier in your grandmother's day.' Magnus said, coming out of the front door.

'I think it's lovely,' Lara said truthfully.

He looked around him and nodded. 'There's colour all year round.'

'Did you have a good trip?' Lara asked.

'Trip?' He looked at her blankly for a moment.

'The fishing,' she said, feeling a bit foolish.

'Oh, yes. Fine, thanks.'

'I saw your mother on Tuesday, while you were both still out. She worries about you both, doesn't she?'

'Aye, she does. But there's no need. Things have changed a lot since my father's time.'

'Have they?' Lara asked doubtfully. 'Listening to the local radio, you wouldn't always think so. There was that ferry fouling its propeller and being escorted into Lerwick; and the fishing boat losing power and being towed home by the lifeboat . . . '

'Ah, but we do have better boats,' Magnus answered, 'and better equipment. Radar, radios — And with all these satellites about, we get more accurate weather forecasts.

'My father was a one-man outfit. He worked for his family, so he went out in all weathers. He had to.'

'It must have been a terrible time for you all when he died,' Lara said softly.

'Aye.' His manner was suddenly abrupt, reminding Lara that, in his opinion, anyone who could ignore their grandmother's existence for twenty-five years would possess none of the finer feelings needed to understand. 'You'd better come inside,' he added in an offhand way.

The house, to Lara's amazement, was spotless. She liked to think of herself as a tidy person but here, there wasn't a single thing out of place. Admittedly, she only caught a glimpse of the kitchen as she followed him to the back of the house, but it gleamed.

He noticed her interest. 'Mum comes in while I'm away and tidies up. I haven't yet worked out if she does it for me, or if she can't bear to think of Granny Sutherland turning in her grave.'

Passing an open door, Lara couldn't help noticing that one room had escaped Shona's ministrations. There were papers spread across a table, two chairs, the wide window-sill, and the floor.

Magnus came back to look over her shoulder. 'I've been trying to sort the accounts out.'

'Why don't you use an accountant?'

'Oh, I do. It's just that I have to sort it all out so the poor fellow can make head or tail of it.'

He took Lara through another door which led into a conservatory.

'Oh, this is lovely!' Lara exclaimed. 'What a view!'

'Looking down over the voe — yes, it's not bad. Moira had this built just after Iain died. It was her pride and joy.'

He gestured to the many boxes piled up by a coffee table. 'Those are full of her things.' He pointed. 'And those are her paintings.'

He picked something out of one of the boxes and handed it to her — a silver photo frame.

Lara looked at the photograph and cringed. Staring back at her was a child with a huge, toothy, self-confident grin. Her blonde hair stuck out at either side in two bunches tied with enormous ribbons. It was the face of a child sure in the knowledge that she was the most important thing in the world.

'What a precocious little brat I looked,' Lara said lightly.

Magnus didn't agree but neither did he argue. 'I'll leave you to it, if that's all right. I've got a lot to do. Shout if you need anything.'

'Yes — thanks.'

As soon as he'd gone, Lara sat down and stared at the photograph. It was awful. And it was all Moira had owned to remind her of her only grandchild.

The thought was an unhappy one, and Lara thrust the photograph aside and opened one of the boxes. It was filled mostly with books, several of which boasted beautifully embroidered bookmarks.

On the top of another box was a thick photograph album, and Lara sat back to study it. Each photograph had a neat caption beneath it. Several were of her mother as a child — 'Meg', each of them dated. Till Shona Cameron used the name, Lara had never heard her mother called anything but 'Margaret'.

There was a photograph of two dark-haired lads in a tiny rowing boat. The man with them, Lara guessed, had to be Robbie, their fisherman father who had drowned . . . Shona's hero.

There was a photograph of Iain, looking young, smart and very dashing in his RAF uniform; Lara's parents on their wedding day; Lara as a baby; a crowd of strangers gathered around a Christmas tree . . .

'Sorry.' Magnus stuck his head round the door. 'Would you like a cup of tea? Or coffee?'

Lara was surprised, and smiled to herself. This had to be Shona's influence. Guests, no matter how unwelcome, should always be offered tea.

'Thanks, but I really couldn't.' She didn't want to put him out. On the other hand, she thought suddenly, she didn't want to appear rude, either. 'I made four home visits earlier, and I had a cup of tea at each house.

'Not that I'm complaining,' she added hastily, before he gave her yet another black mark. 'You discover far more about a patient during a cup of tea and a chat than you do from any examination . . . '

She held out the photograph of himself and Alisdair on the rowing boat. 'Is that your father?'

He gazed at it for a moment or two. 'Yes. Yes, that's Dad.'

'Wouldn't Shona love to have it?' Lara

flushed. 'Sorry — it's yours, Magnus. You probably — and anyway it's none of my business.'

'No, you're right.' His voice was gentle now, and he reached out to take the photo. 'I'm sure Mum would like it. I've never seen it before.'

'You've never looked at these things?' Lara was amazed.

'Not closely. When I bought the cottage 'and contents', I imagined 'contents' to be odd pieces of furniture. I couldn't believe your mother would be so — ' He broke off abruptly. 'Most of the furniture went to a young couple who were getting married but I've no idea what to do with this lot. We don't bring anything into the world and we can't take anything out — ' He shook his head. 'But Moira certainly collected a lot while she was here.'

'One visit isn't going to make much impact.' Lara looked around. 'Unless you have some time to help?'

'Sure.'

He sat down on a chair opposite and looked inside another of the boxes. Lara wondered if he felt, as she did, that they were prying into a life that had had so little contact with her own . . .

It was Magnus, almost an hour later, who

found the letters. There were two of them and, after glancing at them, he handed them to Lara without a word.

They'd been written by Iain during the war.

The first was pitiful, a letter written by a man who had been totally broken by all he'd experienced — by his injuries and the mental damage the war had done to him. It would have been heart-breaking to receive.

The second had been written by a man who had just learnt that he had a daughter. *There have been times, many times, when I've wished that I might die, too, like my friends. Now, in our daughter, you've given me a glimpse of a future worth fighting for. Kiss our dear Margaret for me, and pray that soon the three of us will be together. It's all I live for* . . .

Lara could have wept. Her mother's birth had given Iain hope for the future, and yet it had all gone horribly wrong.

And Moira — how had she felt, receiving that letter, knowing it was all a lie?

'These are too private,' Lara said, her voice husky with emotion.

'I wonder why Moira kept them?' Magnus murmured. 'There must have been others that she didn't keep. She was a very practical woman ... she would have known that someone would read them. I can only suppose that she thought your mother would — Well, perhaps she wanted your mother to read them.'

Lara didn't know. The more real these people became, and the more she learnt of their feelings, the more it upset her. That 'clean break' had been such a tragic waste.

'I would have loved to know her.' She spoke her thoughts aloud, and flushed as she caught his cynical eye.

'I ought to go,' she said abruptly. 'Perhaps I could come back another time?'

'Of course. I'll leave everything — Dear God!' He had stood up, brushed against a box and just managed to save an ornament. 'And I always thought this was plastic!'

It was a glass ball sitting on a wooden plinth. Inside the glass was a small girl walking through a snow-covered pine forest. When it was shaken, as Magnus had done, it gave the effect of a snow storm.

'Moira always kept this well out of reach of young boys' hands.' Magnus cradled it in his strong palms. 'Many times, I saw her shake it and then drift into a world of her own until the snow had settled.'

'It's very beautiful.'

Magnus held it out. 'Take it.'

'Oh, no. I couldn't!'

'Yes,' he insisted. 'It meant a lot to your granny. I'm sure she would have liked you to have it. Anyway, you'll look after it — all I'm likely to do is break it.'

Lara took it from him with hands that trembled. 'Thank you, Magnus.'

Lara drove home and put the ornament on the top shelf of her bookshelf, but long before the snow had settled, her vision was blurred by tears.

★ ★ ★

The following day, Lara experienced one of Shetland's sudden storms. The rain came from nowhere. One minute, she was lifting her camera to take a snap of Scalloway Castle, and the next, she was running for her car.

After a brief hesitation, just long enough to tell herself that she could end up swimming back to her car, she took shelter in the small museum. It was one of the many places she'd planned to visit on rainy days but, so far, there hadn't been too many of those.

It was crammed with exhibits, all of them connected to Scalloway's history. There was a lot concerned with the fishing industry, but Lara was fascinated by the personal items; a gentleman's moustache cup; a beautifully preserved wedding dress.

The rain stopped as suddenly as it had started, and she was about to leave when, at the back of the museum, she saw the name 'Larsen'.

Her heart missed a sudden beat but, on closer inspection, she saw that this was a Lief Larsen, a Norwegian who had received a succession of awards from the British Crown. Apparently, only the fact that as a foreigner, he hadn't been eligible, had prevented him being given the Victoria Cross.

Lief Larsen had been a prime mover in what was called the Shetland Bus. Lara had never heard of it. As she read about the brave men who'd run a shuttle service of small boats between Shetland and Nazi-occupied Norway, she was caught up in the story and didn't hear someone else coming in.

'Fascinating, isn't it?'

The man's voice startled her and she realised belatedly that she was in his way. 'Oh, I'm sorry.' She moved back, smiling. 'Yes, it is. I'm ashamed to say I knew nothing about this.'

'It's hard to imagine what Shetland was like during the war,' the man remarked, 'with troops outnumbering civilians, and Norwegian refugees arriving on a daily basis.'

Lara gazed at the photographs.

'I was here in 'Sixty-seven,' the man went on, 'when about three hundred Norwegian war veterans returned. It was very moving.'

Three hundred! 'My grandmother knew a Norwegian during the war,' Lara told him. 'In my ignorance, I thought a Norwegian would have stuck out like a sore thumb.'

'Hardly.' He chuckled. 'The ties between Shetland and Norway have always been strong, and never more so than during the war.'

'Do you live here?' Lara asked.

'I was born in Lerwick,' he said with a touch of pride. 'My parents moved south when I was twelve, but I keep in touch and visit most years. Actually,' he admitted with a smile, 'I only came in to escape the rain.'

'So did I,' Lara told him, 'but it's so interesting.'

'It's amazing how a small place like this could play such an important part in a war. The best known operation was the Bus, of course, but there was so much more.'

'If you're interested in it,' he said, as he was leaving, 'there's to be a showing of some archive film in town. I leave tomorrow so I didn't pay too much attention but I think it's on Wednesday night. There's a notice down by the slipway.'

'Thanks,' Lara replied. 'I'll have a look at it.'

By Wednesday, though, Lara's favourite cousin would be visiting. She couldn't imagine Fran being too keen to spend an evening watching old home movies.

On her way out, Lara spotted the name Larsen again and had the sinking feeling that it must be the Norwegian equivalent of Smith or Jones. For all she knew, Anders was probably the equivalent of John. Added to that, of course, she now knew that the Norwegians arriving in Shetland had been counted, not in hundreds, but in thousands . . .

No wonder Magnus had mentioned 'a Norwegian' living nearby. There must be dozens who'd settled on this side of the North Sea after the war. Why had she leapt to the conclusion he must mean Anders?

★   ★   ★

Lara met Fran at the airport on Saturday morning, and the rest of the day, and most of the night after dinner with Tony, had been spent catching up on news.

On Sunday morning, Lara drove her cousin around, and in the afternoon, they

76

walked across the white sand to St Ninian's Isle.

Then they drove to Lerwick, and sat on the wall of the harbour eating hot, filled tatties while they waited for Tony to join them. Other people were eating fish and chips, while hopeful herring gulls kept a watching eye on them.

'These birds must have a terrible diet,' Fran said with a laugh.

'Unlike us.' Lara smiled. 'What with Tony taking us to dinner later, and invitations from Shona for tomorrow night and Pat for Tuesday night — '

'Pat?'

'Pat Rendall,' Lara reminded her. 'My partner's wife. You'll like her.'

'People here are so friendly, aren't they?' Fran mused. 'After speaking to your mum — well, she painted a very different picture of Shetlanders.'

'But, Lara, she did talk about *when* they visit, not if. I asked her when it would be, and she said as soon as your dad could arrange time away from the office.'

Lara refused to raise her hopes. 'I'll believe it when I see it,' she said, throwing her tattie skin to a gull which at once swooped on it with a raucous cry.

'Oh, and I nearly forgot,' Fran added with

a grin. 'Gran says your phone calls are most welcome, and the postcards are very informative, but what's happened to the letters?'

'I've been promising her a letter for ages.' Lara chuckled. 'Her last letter was eight pages long. Perhaps when we've been to see this house. I'll tell her all about that.'

'What does Tony think about it?'

'He thinks I'm being a bit premature,' Lara admitted. 'He says it's too soon to buy a place in case it doesn't work out up here. But I feel as if I belong here. I want a place of my own.'

'He hasn't suggested that you buy a place together?'

Lara looked at her. 'He's not ready for that.'

'Oh, Lara, what rubbish. You're bound to get married sooner or later. This seems like the ideal time . . .'

'He's not ready,' Lara said again, 'and I haven't suggested it. I don't want to push him.'

'Perhaps he *needs* a push. What about you? If he did ask you to marry him — '

'I'd throw caution to the wind and drag him off to church before he changed his mind,' Lara admitted.

'There's hardly any caution to throw to the wind,' Fran retorted dryly. 'You've been together for ever. What you don't know about each other now, you never will know.'

'But what if — for instance — Tony wanted to move back to London and I wanted to stay here?' Lara asked.

'Then you'd work out a compromise.' Fran sounded patient, which meant she was impatient. 'That's what marriage is all about.'

'Tony's been through such a lot. I just feel he needs time to settle into his new life.'

'Perhaps when he sees you in a place of your own?' Fran murmured. 'I wonder what this house is like inside, don't you?'

Lara had driven past it twice before getting the details from the agent. Then she'd driven past it again, and made an appointment to have a look round.

'It's where it's built that I've fallen in love with. I really wanted an older place — this was only built fifteen years ago. It's such a lovely spot, though, with the hill at the back and the house looking down on to the voe. Anyway, we'll find out tomorrow.'

The junior members of the sailing club were taking their boats out and they watched them sail into the Sound.

Lara was watching the ferry go out when she spotted Alisdair. He waved and came over.

'How are you liking Shetland, Fran?' he asked, after Lara had made the introductions.

'I love it! I only arrived yesterday but we've been all over the place today. We saw the puffins at Sumburgh Head, and then walked across to St Ninian's Isle.'

He sat on the wall beside them. 'I've been trying to convince Lara that she'd see far more from a boat.'

'Without any success, I might add,' Lara put in.

'It would be lovely,' Fran said immediately. 'Lara, you should. As a doctor, there could be times when you *have* to go on a boat.'

Lara was well aware of that.

'If I had to go, then, of course, I'd go. But it's not something I'd do for pleasure. Perhaps we'll take the ferry to Bressay,' she added as a concession.

The others laughed at this.

'Perhaps we'll forget the ferry and swim across,' Fran retorted with a grin. 'How far is it? Half a mile?'

'Three-quarters,' Alisdair said. 'Work on her, Fran. We'll have a trip round Bressay and Noss on the *Shearwater*. That's our boat.

'Meanwhile — ' He glanced at his watch. 'I've got to go. Did Mum say we'd see you both tomorrow night?'

'She did,' Lara replied.

'Good, I'll see you both then.'

Alisdair walked away, waving before he

turned the corner and was gone.

'I've died and gone to heaven.' Fran sighed. 'No, if this were heaven, I wouldn't be wearing this awful skirt.'

'Sorry?'

'Lara! You've told me every detail of your meeting with Magnus, Shona and then Alisdair. For some reason, you neglected to mention the fact that Alisdair is absolutely gorgeous.'

'Alisdair?' Lara gaped at her.

'You haven't noticed?'

'Well — '

'You're not married yet, you know.' Fran giggled. 'You're still entitled to look!'

'I do look.' Lara grinned. 'And Alisdair is — '

'Gorgeous!'

Lara thought about it for a moment.

'He and Magnus are very similar in looks. They're both tall, both dark, and both very fit looking. And I think that's it — Alisdair's bursting with good health, and blessed with a permanent smile. It's his sunny personality that makes him seem so attractive.'

'Personality!' Fran rolled her eyes.

'Mind you,' Lara went on, 'you're not alone. According to Shona, he's had more than his fair share of girlfriends.'

'I'm not surprised.' Fran looked wicked. 'If

I were here for longer than a week — '

'The novelty would wear off,' Lara assured her. 'I expect Alisdair's interest in the interior design business is only equalled by your interest in the price of fish!'

Fran didn't argue.

'And here comes someone else who's gorgeous,' she said with a smile.

Lara looked up and saw Tony striding towards them.

'Now there I have to agree with you, Fran.'

She found herself looking at Tony as if for the first time. It was a long time since she'd fallen for his good looks and, these days, she rarely gave his appearance a second thought. Above all, she loved the way he was with people. He'd always been a good doctor but, since Jane's death, he was even more caring. He could put any patient at their ease and he never failed to understand, no matter how trivial the complaint, how anxious a patient was feeling. He made Lara feel equally confident, as if nothing bad could happen, as if there was nothing in the world to worry about . . .

He was heading their way, when he caught up with a girl and stopped to talk to her.

'Who's that?' Fran asked.

'I've no idea.'

The girl was in her mid-twenties, Lara

supposed, with short, dark hair. They talked for a few minutes, or rather the girl talked and Tony listened. Then she placed a hand on Tony's arm, said something that made him smile, and carried on her way.

Tony watched her for a moment before walking over to join Lara and Fran.

He kissed Lara briefly and sat on the wall beside her. 'Had a good day?'

'Wonderful!' Fran enthused.

'You?' Lara asked.

'Very good.' He looked at the busy scene around them and added with satisfaction, 'London seems a long way away, doesn't it?' Without waiting for a reply, he went on. 'So make me envious and tell me about your day.'

While Fran did just that, Lara sat quiet, her hand in Tony's. She wished that she and Tony were planning ahead, looking at houses together, thinking of a family, looking forward to growing old together . . .

★ ★ ★

Lara had tolerated a great deal of leg pulling about the archive film show, but as she, Fran and Tony entered the hall on Wednesday evening, she knew that they were as intrigued as she was. They all wanted to see what Shetland had been like during the war.

83

The place was already crowded and they took seats near the back. People chatted around them but Lara was engrossed in her own thoughts.

She wasn't sure what she hoped to gain from seeing this film. One thing was certain, it was the story of the Shetland Bus and, as such, the story of some of the Norwegians who had come to Shetland during the war. Perhaps, seeing them, she would go home with an idea of the type of man her grandfather must have been.

Fran nudged her. 'Isn't that Alisdair?'

Lara looked across. Sure enough, three rows from the front sat Alisdair and Magnus, with a white head between them. Shona was nowhere to be seen.

'It's strange they didn't say they were coming,' Fran said.

'They probably didn't think we'd be interested. Good job I dragged you along,' Lara teased. 'You and Alisdair will be able to discuss it tomorrow.'

Alisdair had invited them both for a trip on the *Shearwater* in the morning. Fortunately, Lara was on duty, but she was pleased that Fran would be entertained.

'Have you thought any more about the house?' Tony said into her right ear.

'All the time!' She turned to him eagerly.

'It's got everything I want — superb views, plenty of space, a garden that's easy to manage, a big kitchen — and that conservatory!'

He laughed. 'All right, calm down! You like it. So will you buy it?'

'Every time I think I'll buy it, I think of the expense. I hadn't planned on anything quite so expensive. It's not the mortgage so much as the furniture I'll need. What do you think?'

'It's handy for the surgery,' Tony answered thoughtfully. 'I really don't know, Lara. It has to be your decision. I suppose you can always sell it if things don't work out.'

'That's right,' Lara agreed. 'I could look upon it as an investment. I really want a place of my own, Tony. I want a garden, and somewhere I can be myself, without worrying about scratching the furniture.'

'Yes, I know exactly what you mean. It's just that if you waited — ' He paused. 'Perhaps one day we'll want to buy a place together — '

His voice trailed away.

'Don't let my mother catch you saying that,' Lara teased, hiding her feelings.

Smiling, he shook his head. 'She knows it's too soon for that.'

Don't you believe it, Lara thought with an inner sigh.

Across the hall, she caught sight of the girl Tony had stopped to talk to at the harbour. 'Isn't that your friend?'

He looked and then nodded.

'Her name's Anna Thompson. Her grandfather brought her up, and she's taken his death very hard. That's why she'd been to the clinic.'

Lara felt ridiculously pleased that he'd met Anna through his work. But just then a hush fell on the audience, and a man welcomed them to the hall. Lara was soon caught up in the story of the Shetland Bus and the men who had escaped from occupied Norway in their tiny fishing boats. When these boats returned to the Norwegian coast and safely brought back more refugees, the idea was formed that radio transmitters, explosives and weapons, messengers and radio operators, could be sent to the underground movement in Norway by the same means.

Lara shuddered at the size of the boats, some only fifty feet long. She wouldn't want a trip round Lerwick's harbour in one, but some of these crossings were over a thousand miles and with explosives, weapons, radios and radio operators on board.

What made it worse was that, to escape the watchful eyes of the Germans, the trips had to be carried out in darkness. With little darkness so far north during the summer months, this meant that the trips had to be made during the winter when the sea was at its roughest.

Everyone in the hall was intent on the old film footage. A group of smiling faces came onto the screen . . .

'Lara!' Fran gasped, and Lara felt Tony's hand grip hers tightly.

The face had gone from the screen, but it was crystal clear in Lara's mind. For a second, she had been looking at someone who could have been her twin — except that the young man would now be in his seventies.

'Lara, that's astounding! He was so like you,' Tony murmured. Lara felt her heart, threatening to burst out of her ribcage, could surely be heard.

She glanced quickly at Tony's shocked face but then turned away, needing to keep her eyes on the screen. The young man didn't appear again, though a laughing group of local girls appeared at the very end of the film, with some of the Bus crews.

As soon as the film ended, and people began to talk amongst themselves or leave the hall, Lara removed her still-trembling hand from Tony's and got to her feet.

'I'll be back in a minute,' she told them

both. 'I need to see Magnus.'

Magnus would have seen that face, too. If it was Anders Larsen — and it must have been — didn't it stand to reason that Magnus had known the man?

'You're the image of your grandfather,' he'd said the first time he met her, and she was certainly the image of that young man. His face had almost leapt out of the screen at her.

She made her way to the front of the hall. It was neither the time nor the place to confront Magnus, but she had to know the truth.

Magnus and his brother were still seated, talking to the elderly man who was sitting between them. Lara hesitated, but then decided to interrupt them.

As the elderly gentleman looked up, she froze on the spot.

The three of them stood up and the man turned towards Lara.

He was a total stranger, and yet the blue-grey eyes which were taking in her every feature were the same eyes Lara saw whenever she looked into a mirror.

She looked at his hands; those strong, loving hands she'd remembered that day at the beach. His presence had filled her with such powerful feelings of safety, trust and love that, a quarter of a century later, the memory still remained.

A total stranger — but she knew without doubt that this was Anders Larsen, her grandfather.

4

Lara had to bite back a cry as Anders Larsen moved carefully towards her. She'd expected to see him standing tall and strong, proud and happy — just as he had in the film.

But her grandfather was stooped and frail. The effort of standing had taken the colour from his thin face, leaving only a sickening, tell-tale grey. Lara knew that pallor all too well, from her training years in hospital. She could hear every painful, rasping breath he took.

His eyes on Lara's, Anders staggered for a moment. Magnus was quick to offer a steadying arm, before he and his brother looked to see what it was that had so shocked the old man. Alisdair's face, as open as ever, registered pure surprise. Magnus looked very grim indeed.

Lara knew exactly what Magnus was thinking and she could only echo his thoughts. She wasn't sure what Anders was seeing, but she knew that the timing couldn't have been worse. Anders was still wrapped up in the film. He was caught up in the past.

Lara walked towards them. Her heart was

racing and her head whirling. The doctor in her could see how sick this man was, but she couldn't hold back, not now that they were in the same room together after so long. If she'd thought for one moment that her grandfather might be at the film show — but, of course, she hadn't.

She was aware of glances from folk around her, of quiet nudges and talk. She saw Magnus, clearly worried, tighten his grip on Anders' arm. But she couldn't look away from those elderly, confused blue eyes. Anders seemed to be checking to see if Lara was real, or just a figment of his overworked mind.

Magnus increased his hold on Anders' arm and bent slightly to speak to him. 'This is Doctor Daniels, Anders. She's the new GP — George's new partner.'

If Anders heard or understood what Magnus said, he gave no indication of having done so.

Lara was close enough now to reach out and clasp his hands in hers.

'Moira?' he said. His voice was weak and husky.

'No.' Lara's eyes filled with tears, and she blinked them away. 'I'm Lara. Moira's granddaughter. Look — let's sit down, till this rush for the doors is over.'

Anders sank gratefully into the nearest seat, and Lara sat by his side.

'Are you OK, Anders?' Alisdair asked with quiet concern.

Lara could feel the tremors shuddering through Anders' hands, and every breath he took hurt her as it did him.

'He'll be fine,' she told Alisdair with a reassuring smile. 'It's hot and stuffy in here. He'll be fine in a moment.'

He wouldn't, of course.

She rubbed his cold hands. Many times, she'd seen visitors to the hospital rubbing the hands of their loved ones, trying to transfer some of their own life and vitality.

The hands she held now were no longer the strong, protective hands she'd held as a child. They were weak and frail . . . Suddenly, the feelings she'd had looking out over the voe, her first week here, came flooding back. When she was little, Anders had been allowed to get to know her, to take her out! For them both, this was a reunion.

While Anders struggled to regain his composure, Lara held his hands. She tried to ignore the murmured comments and whispers as people made their slow way to the doors.

Magnus and Alisdair were having a whispered argument.

'I'll go and fetch the car, shall I?' Alisdair suggested uncertainly.

His brother, watching over Anders, didn't reply.

'Good idea,' Lara murmured.

Her grandfather's breathing was easier, and she could feel his pulse rate slowing.

'Feeling better?' she asked.

He nodded, and managed a feeble smile.

Lara wasn't fooled. She knew how much this was costing him. His energy levels were just about exhausted. Seeing himself — and Moira — as they had been, and then having the shock of seeing her . . .

'Alisdair's gone for the car,' she told him. 'You'll soon be home.'

'Yes.' Just one word and the effort was immense. His fingers curled around hers, and huge pools formed in blue eyes that were flecked with grey.

Lara had always thought that she'd inherited her eyes from her father . . . hers, too, had those grey flecks in them.

'I'm sorry,' Anders said hoarsely.

'Shut up, man!' Magnus muttered, putting his hand on his shoulder.

Lara couldn't speak for the choking lump that had wedged itself in her throat.

'Is everything all right?'

What a relief to hear Tony's voice, the tone

Lara thought of as his doctor's voice, calm, steady, and reassuring.

'Tony, this is — ' Lara swallowed and tried again. 'This is Anders Larsen.'

Tony put his arm round her shoulders. He knew exactly who it was.

'He was feeling a bit shaky for a moment,' Lara explained. 'It's far too hot in here. Alisdair's bringing the car round.'

'I'm Tony Adams,' he introduced himself. 'Lara's friend.'

Anders clearly wasn't taking that in. His eyes were fixed on Lara's, still.

Alisdair appeared at the door. They were the only people left in the hall now, and Magnus put a hand below Anders' arm. 'Come on, Anders, the car's here. Let's get you home.'

Anders looked to Lara, clearly unwilling to leave her.

'Yes, that's right,' Lara said gently. 'I'll come and see you soon, I promise. Magnus will take you home now.'

'Come on, Anders,' Magnus said, and this time his voice was insistent.

Without releasing his hands, Lara rose, and then helped Magnus to get the old man smoothly to his feet.

'I'll see you soon,' she promised.

He smiled at her, slowly, warmly.

'Yes, Lara. Make it soon.'

He swayed a little, and she leaned forward to support him. Impulsively, she kissed his cheek, and stood back to watch each painfully slow step that took her grandfather out of the hall. Magnus was walking by Anders' side with his hands clenched tightly behind his back, as if that was the only way he could stop himself from offering unwanted help.

The weight of Tony's arm around her shoulders was comforting. Outwardly, Lara was composed, but inside, her heart was breaking.

Of all the memories that coming to Shetland might have evoked, Lara had only one. Just one very clear memory of a man who had held her hand.

The child she was had known instinctively that the man had loved her. She had been far too young to question it, but she had known. Now, twenty-five years later, the love was still there, stronger than ever, and she could recognise it for what it was. This was a love that cared nothing for what she was, what she did, or what she thought. It was a love that forgave anything and everything. It was an unconditional love, a love born long, long ago.

And now, just when she had found him, she was going to lose him all over again.

Anders Larsen had, she knew, only a short time to live . . .

*　*　*

The following afternoon, Lara sat on the stone wall, the nearest thing to seating that her garden offered, and tried to coax herself into action.

She was unsuccessful. She made the mistake of closing her eyes against the bright sun and she was almost asleep when Tony stopped his car in the drive.

A sense of longing swept over her as he strode towards her. Since coming to Shetland, Lara's life had been turned completely upside down, but at the centre of it all was Tony, never changing.

'You look awful,' he said, sitting on the wall beside her. 'Rough day?'

'Probably no worse than usual.' Lara thought about it and added, 'Actually, I think it was. I've never seen so many trivial ailments in my life. All those years of training and I end up handing out ointments for insect bites.'

'This is want you wanted, Lara.' Tony reminded her.

'I know. And it's still what I want. It's just that — '

'You feel yourself to be above insect bites?'

Lara was forced to laugh. 'Yes, I do!'

She slipped her arm through his and rested her head on his shoulder. 'I'm glad you're here. Fran's driven into Scalloway to visit the knitwear shop. To be honest, I wasn't sorry. I thought I wanted to be alone. What I really wanted, though, was for you to cheer me up.'

'You should have called me.' His fingers lightly stroked her hair. 'Mind you, I've been rushed off my feet.' He smiled. 'It's all relative though, isn't it? Compared to the days we had back home, I suppose it's been fairly quiet.'

Back home. Whenever he spoke of London, it was always 'home', where Lara felt now that *this* was 'home'. There were ties, most of them invisible, that bound her more tightly to these islands than she would have believed possible.

'Anna Thompson rang me.' Tony interrupted her thoughts.

Lara sat up. 'Why?'

'Because I was the one who suggested she see her GP. Anyway, she said she felt much better after talking to you.'

Anna hadn't mentioned that she'd visited the surgery on Tony's advice, but perhaps she didn't realise that the two doctors knew each other.

'She's very generous then, because I made a right hash of that, too. She almost walked out in disgust.'

'No,' Tony contradicted her. 'She almost walked out because she thought she was wasting your time.'

He was probably right, Lara supposed, but that didn't forgive the offhand remark she'd made when Anna had suggested she might need a tonic. 'I'm worried about her, Tony. She's very depressed.'

'Yes, I know. But she has to be tougher than she looks. If she can cope with someone suffering from Alzheimer's, she can cope with anything.'

Lara wasn't so sure. 'Did you get to know her well while her grandfather was in hospital?'

'Not really. She always seemed very busy and well organised. She was never late visiting her grandfather. You could set your watch by her . . . Then, when he died, she seemed to go to pieces.'

'I've started at the bottom,' Lara explained, 'hoping that if I can make sure she gets some sleep, she'll start the day on a more even keel. I'm going to see her on Monday, and I've made her promise to get out and see people. I've suggested that new group for one-parent families.'

'One-parent families?' Tony repeated with a puzzled frown.

'Yes. For years, she's looked after her grandfather and her daughter but now she feels — '

'Daughter?'

'You didn't know?'

Tony shook his head. 'I didn't even know she was married.'

'She isn't. That's one of the problems. The father met someone else and abandoned her before they could get around to marriage. But there's more to it than that, a lot more. She had to shut herself off to take care of her grandfather and now that he's gone, she feels — Oh, I don't know. Useless, I suppose. And the poor thing's exhausted.'

Tony dropped a gentle kiss on her forehead. 'I still say she's tougher than she looks. And I know she's in safe hands.'

He gazed into her troubled eyes. 'But the way you're feeling has nothing to do with Anna, or insect bites, does it?'

'No.' He could read her like a book. 'No, it's Anders — my grandfather. Saying that is quite a thrill, you know? I just have this one memory of him — it must have been the last time my parents brought me up here — and I didn't even know it was him . . . '

He took her in his arms. 'You know he

hasn't got long, love? It's lung cancer.'

'I know,' she said soberly. 'Unmistakable. It makes it worse, Tony, that I haven't known him up till now. Last night — ' she broke off.

'I was bowled over,' Tony said. 'Looking at the two of you together — you're so alike, Lara. Two proud, stubborn . . . ' His voice failed him for a moment, and Lara buried her head in his shoulder.

'How long would you say he has?' she asked, her voice muffled.

'You know yourself, Lara. Months, at most.' His arms tightened round her. 'Hell! Here's your car. Fran's back from her shopping trip.'

He lifted her chin. 'You OK?'

'Yes.'

She put a smile in place for her cousin. 'They hadn't sold it then?' she said, nodding at the bulging carrier in Fran's hand.

'No. In fact, I bought two!'

She knelt on the grass in front of them and opened the bag. Crammed inside were two thick jumpers, one in warm shades of autumn, and the other in all the colours of the rainbow.

'This was the one I saw yesterday.' Fran held the more muted one against her. 'Then I saw this one, and I thought it would be perfect for brightening up a dull, grey London winter.'

Lara made suitable comments but her mind was elsewhere. 'Fran, when you were out on the *Shearwater* this morning, did Alisdair say anything about Anders?'

'Not a thing.' Fran folded the jumpers. 'And to be honest, I forgot all about it. We had such a magical morning. It was lovely on the boat.'

She laughed at Lara's doubtful expression. 'You would have enjoyed it. We even had some seals following us. Then, after lunch, Alisdair showed me over their fishing boat, the *Ermingerd*.'

'Is that theirs?' Lara asked in amazement. 'I've seen that in the harbour. It's massive.'

'It's quite comfy. I wouldn't mind a few days on that.'

Lara groaned. 'I can think of nothing worse. And what or where is Ermingerd?'

Fran thought for a moment. 'I've no idea.'

Two gulls landed on the wall a short distance from them. Then, after making a great deal of noise, they flew off in opposite directions.

They sat on in the sunshine, companionably silent. Tony's arm was still a pleasant weight round Lara's shoulders, and she leaned against him.

'I think I'll go and see Anders tomorrow.' She voiced her thoughts.

Fran looked up. 'Oh, Lara. Are you sure?'

'You think I should leave it a while?'

Her cousin was silent for a moment.

'He's very ill — you said so yourself. Meeting you upset him. I honestly can't see any good coming from it.'

Lara was shocked. If the circumstances had been reversed, Lara would have expected to see Fran on his doorstep that very morning.

'You don't think I should see him again?'

'No,' Fran said. 'I don't. Leave things be, Lara. You'll only upset him again, and yourself.'

Lara struggled to make sense of this piece of advice. It was so unlike Fran. They always thought the same way. Always. Surely Fran, of all people, must understand that she *had* to see him.

Tony, Lara noticed, was keeping silent on the subject.

'What do you think?' she asked him.

His answer was a long time coming. 'I know you're longing to talk to him, and he made it clear last night that he wanted to see you again.'

'But, Tony, he was so shaken by it all,' Fran argued. Turning to Lara, she said urgently, 'Don't you think you're being selfish? You've

102

no idea what happened in the past, Lara. You don't know what memories you might be stirring up. Can't you just leave well alone?'

The words stung. Lara was too hurt to answer. She stood up, shaking Tony's arm away. 'I'll see about getting us something to eat.'

'Oh, Lara.' Fran's voice was full of apology. 'I didn't mean — '

'That's OK,' Lara cut her off. 'I expect you're both hungry. What would anyone like?'

'I'll get something,' Fran offered quietly. 'You've been working all day. Better still, let's go out. My treat.' In a teasing voice she added, 'Nothing personal, love, but your cooking has never been noted for its originality.'

Lara smiled but a great gulf had opened up between them. It was the first time her cousin — close as any sister — had disagreed with her about something so vital.

'It's just as well,' Tony said lightly. 'If she could cook on top of everything else, someone would have snapped her up years ago.'

'I'll go and change,' Fran said, not looking at Lara. 'You two can decide where you want to eat. No expense spared.'

As she hurried inside, Lara was gazing out at a small boat heading for the salmon cages.

She could just make out the salmon as they broke the surface. It was a restful scene, one that never failed to please her.

'Why is Fran so against me seeing Anders?'

'Because she cares about you,' Tony answered simply. 'As I do. She doesn't understand the bond between you, any more than I do. I'm just afraid of what Anders might be going to tell you.

'For all you know, he might have hurt Moira badly. And then there's your mum, darling. If he's responsible for the rift between your mum and the Sutherlands, he's caused a great deal of heartache for all concerned.'

'You think I don't know that?' Lara snapped. She threw up her hands. 'Why is everyone treating me like a child?'

She was all set to march inside but Tony was on his feet in an instant. His hand shot out and he grabbed her wrist, turning her round. 'Hey, this is me. Tony. Remember?'

She stood stiffly, refusing to relax against him.

'You will get hurt, darling. If he's responsible for all the heartache, that will hurt. If he's the man you want him to be, you won't have enough time to get to know him, and that will hurt. If he's responsible for your never knowing Moira — '

Silent tears fell on to Lara's cheeks. Tony tried to brush them away but more followed.

He gathered her into his arms and as he caressed her soft hair, he could feel her tears soaking through his shirt.

'Hush, darling,' he whispered. 'We'll work it out, somehow. I'll be right here . . .'

★　★　★

Shona Cameron checked the vegetables again, checked the clock on the kitchen wall, and then heard two cars pull into the drive, one after the other. She should have known her sons would arrive in time to eat.

She hadn't seen either of them all day, and they were away to sea in the morning. It was lucky they had good appetites, she decided, otherwise she'd see nothing of them at all.

As they walked into the kitchen, Alisdair was laughing heartily at something. Magnus, Shona noticed, wasn't even smiling.

Before she could mention this, Alisdair had helped himself to a large slice of fruit-cake from the tin, biting into it eagerly.

'You'll ruin your appetite,' Shona scolded.

'Nonsense,' he retorted with a grin.

Fifteen minutes later, as Shona was putting food in front of them, she thought again how unusually quiet Magnus was.

Alisdair went at his food as if he'd been starved for a week.

'I had lunch too early,' he explained. 'I took Fran after we'd brought the *Shearwater* in.'

Shona had forgotten he was taking Fran out. 'Did she enjoy herself?'

Smiling, Alisdair nodded. 'We had a lot of fun.'

'It was a bonnie morning,' Shona said.

'Perfect.'

Magnus was doing very little with his food, other than rearranging it on his plate.

'What about you, Magnus?' Shona asked. 'What have you been doing all day?'

'I spent the morning with Anders,' he replied. 'I thought I'd call and see if he was OK. He seemed all right, but he had people calling the whole time I was there.'

'Why shouldn't he be all right?' Shona asked with a frown. Then, before he could explain, she guessed. 'It was that film, wasn't it? Oh, Magnus, I told you it would be too much for him. And what's the point of reliving it all?'

'It had nothing to do with the film,' Magnus answered firmly. 'He enjoyed it, and quite right too. It was the Shetland Bus story, so it's not a case of reliving it. It's more a celebration. Any man who was a part of that has a right to feel proud.'

'So if it wasn't the film?'

'Lara!'

Shona looked thoughtfully at her elder son. 'Lara was there?'

'She was,' Magnus confirmed grimly. 'She just appeared from nowhere. When Anders saw her, he had the shock of his life. I don't think he knew where he was.'

'What happened?' Shona asked anxiously.

'Anders got very upset, that's what happened.' His voice rose. 'Why she had to — he'd just seen himself on the screen, looking young, fit and healthy. Then she appeared looking — well . . . I could see Moira in her, last night. Moira was in the crowd in one of those films . . . And she has his eyes . . . '

Shona nodded slowly. 'She's certainly the image of him.'

'So what should have been a pleasant night out for him ended in disaster,' Magnus went on. 'And all thanks to Lara Daniels.'

'It wasn't a disaster at all,' Alisdair argued calmly. 'In fact, it was all very touching. The rest of us might not have existed.'

'What did she say to him?' Shona was sorry now that she hadn't gone herself.

'Nothing really,' Alisdair answered thoughtfully. 'I think they were too shocked to say much. Lara was trying to put Anders at his ease.'

'She kept on about how hot it was in the hall,' Magnus put in.

'Hot? That's a first.' Shona murmured. 'I always take an extra sweater there.'

'And you would have needed it,' Magnus said flatly. 'It was as cold as it always is.'

'She was trying to put Anders at his ease,' Alisdair explained patiently. 'She was making excuses for him, trying to make him feel better.'

'That poor wee lassie,' Shona said softly. 'What a terrible shock it must have been for her, to see him like that.'

'Poor wee lassie?' Magnus exploded. 'What about Anders?'

'He was OK,' Alisdair insisted. 'If it hadn't been for you almost dragging him away, and Lara helping you, he'd still be with her now.'

He looked at his mother. 'A lot of folk noticed what was going on, Mum. They had no need for words. They both seemed to know that they'd found each other, and nothing else mattered.' He smiled at the memory. 'It was very touching.'

'It wasn't so touching when we got him home,' Magnus reminded him.

'He was a bit shaken, that's all.'

'Aye,' Magnus said dryly. 'Just a bit shaken.

Just enough to make him think he'd seen Jakob.'

'He was confused,' Alisdair agreed.

'In the thirty-five years I've known him,' Magnus said quietly, 'he's mentioned Jakob's name no more than half a dozen times. Jakob was his older brother and he died during the war when one of the boats coming from Norway went down. And that's all I know about him. Yet last night, Anders was insisting he'd seen him.'

He sighed loudly. 'And just when he was looking so much better.'

'Magnus,' Shona said gently, 'he's not going to get better, love.'

'I know.' Magnus looked down at his plate. 'You'd think he could be allowed to live what little time he's got left in peace though. Is that too much to ask?'

Shona and Alisdair exchanged a glance, and Magnus went on, oblivious.

'I wish I'd never heard of Lara Daniels. Even living half a world away she managed to make Moira's life a misery. Now she's all set to do the same to Anders.

'Oh, I'll admit that when she looked at Moira's things, and when she took the glass snowstorm — '

He stopped and was silent for a few moments, lost in the memory.

'But what does that prove?' he demanded of them both. 'She didn't do anything for Moira when she was alive and it's too late now that she's dead. I don't know what brought her here but I wish to God it hadn't. She's trouble. You mark my words!'

Shona was speechless. She'd noticed that Magnus was a little reserved where Lara was concerned, but she'd had no idea that his feelings were so strong. It was so unlike her strong, silent elder son.

'You know exactly what brought her here,' Alisdair told his brother quietly. 'She told you herself. Tony came here and she followed him.'

Magnus shrugged.

'She's very attractive, too,' Alisdair added thoughtfully.

Magnus frowned. 'What the devil does that have to do with anything?'

'I don't know,' Alisdair admitted. 'But I do know that something about Lara is getting you steamed up like no other lass has ever got you steamed up before.'

'I am not steamed up!' Magnus retorted.

At Alisdair's unconvinced expression, he added, 'And if I am, it's because she comes here with her too-good-to-be-true, caring ways, and everyone falls for her as if she's God's personal gift to the islands.'

'Mmm,' Alisdair murmured, 'and anyone could be forgiven for thinking that *you've* fallen for her more than most.'

Magnus glared at him. 'What? She's not my type, is she?'

'I wouldn't know,' Alisdair taunted. 'I've yet to work out what your type is.'

'Believe me, she's not it,' Magnus assured his brother. 'Anyway, she'll soon be married to Tony Adams.'

'Did I detect a touch of jealousy there?'

Before Magnus could give vent to words as furious as the expression on his face, Shona spoke calmly.

'Do you think they will get married? Do you think she loves him?'

A sudden spark burned in Magnus' eyes. It vanished almost immediately, but it left Shona feeling chilled.

'She'll marry him,' he said. 'Didn't she say that she was eight years old when she decided to become a doctor? I expect that, at the same time, she decided to marry a doctor, have two point four children and live happily ever after.

'She'll marry him. Love won't come into it.'

Shona regarded him closely. There was no emotion in his voice. Whatever it was she'd seen in his eyes — perhaps she'd imagined it.

'From what Fran said,' Alisdair remarked,

'I gathered that Lara would marry him tomorrow. It's Tony who's delaying. Although I can't see why.'

'That's understandable,' Shona said. 'His first wife was killed, remember.' In an effort to change the subject, she added lightly, 'Are you going to eat that, Magnus?'

'Yes, of course.' Magnus looked at his still-full plate. 'No. Sorry, Mum, I'm not very hungry.'

Alisdair grinned. 'It must be love.'

Their mother didn't catch the muttered curse as Magnus stood up. Judging by the fury on his face as he stopped his chair from hitting the floor, it was probably just as well.

'Magnus, calm down,' Shona coaxed.

'I am calm!' he retorted. 'But I'm hanged if I'll stop and listen to this rubbish!'

'Magnus, stay!'

His hand was already on the door. He turned and shook his head. 'I've got a million things to do. Jimmy's ill, so I need to see Ivan. The way things are going, the *Ermingerd* won't be going anywhere tomorrow.'

He was about to say something else but, after a stony glare in Alisdair's direction, he left, closing the door none too quietly behind him.

'Oh, Ally,' Shona groaned. 'What a stupid thing to say. Whatever possessed you?'

'*He* did.' Alisdair replied. 'He disliked Lara before he met her and now, come hell or high water, he refuses to have a good word for her.'

'It's Anders. You know how he feels about him.' Shona sighed. 'He's different from you, Ally. He feels things more deeply.

'When your dad died, Magnus got it into his head that our family was *his* responsibility. He was barely fourteen, far too young for any of that. You tagged after him like a shadow. He was looking after you, and looking after me.'

'Yes, I know,' Alisdair said quietly, his voice tinged with regret.

'Moira had practically adopted the pair of you, anyway,' Shona went on. 'but that was the only place where Magnus could be himself. With us, he thought he had to be strong and brave. With Moira, he knew he didn't. He was very close to her, and anything that hurt Moira hurt Magnus.

'And it's exactly the same with Anders. At fourteen, Magnus suddenly had nothing in common with other children. Anders was working and living over here half the year. Because he took an interest, Anders became everything to him; father, grandfather, friend. Magnus is very possessive about him.'

'Yes, I know,' Alisdair agreed quietly. 'He's my big brother and I love him dearly

. . . You're right, I shouldn't have said those things. But if he hadn't got so wound up, I wouldn't have egged him on.'

Shona knew that. 'You don't think there's anything in it, do you? His feelings for Lara, I mean?'

Alisdair thought for a moment. 'I don't know,' he said at last. 'He's definitely touchy on the subject.'

Shona longed to dismiss the whole idea as nonsense, but she remembered again the brief flicker of emotion she'd seen in her son's eyes, and the flat, toneless voice as he'd spoken of Lara marrying Tony.

'It would be just like him,' she said shakily. 'All those girls he might have shown an interest in — but no, Magnus would have to fall for someone who's totally out of his reach.'

Alisdair touched her shoulder reassuringly. 'He's not the first man to fall for someone else's girl, and he'll not be the last.'

'Don't!' Shona felt wretched now.

'Stop fretting, Mum,' Alisdair said briskly. 'He's more than big enough to take care of himself.'

His words did nothing to reassure Shona. In fact, they had quite the opposite effect.

'You know what they say, Ally. The bigger they are, the harder they fall.'

5

Lara slowed the car as she spotted her grandfather, standing still, looking painfully frail.

She stopped the car, jumped out and crossed the road. 'Are you all right?'

'Yes, yes. Just — resting.'

'Come and sit in the car.' Lara took his arm, giving him no chance to argue.

Sitting in the passenger seat, his breathing became quieter and more controlled.

'I've been putting flowers on your grandmother's grave,' he said at last. 'Shona usually takes me, or the lads if they're home, but sometimes — ' His eyes closed. He looked exhausted.

'You like to be alone? Even so, it's too far to walk!'

He looked at her, wry amusement in his eyes. 'It didn't seem so far when I was sitting in my kitchen.'

'I've just come from your house.'

'You came to see me?' He looked delighted and Lara was relieved.

'Suppose we go to my place and have a cup of tea?' she suggested.

'I'd like that. Very much.'

It was there again, Lara realised. The feeling that they belonged together, that they had always been together. There was no awkwardness between them; they might have been apart for ten minutes instead of most of her lifetime.

Lara stopped the car outside Little Bay and they walked inside, Anders' painfully slow steps breaking her heart.

'You sit down,' Lara told him, 'and I'll make us some tea.'

When she carried the tray into the sitting-room, Anders was gazing at the glass snowstorm. The snow had almost settled.

She walked over to him and as he turned to look her, Lara was horrified to see tears in those blue-grey eyes.

She slipped her arm through his. 'Come and sit down.'

Lara helped him to the chair. 'Magnus gave me the snowstorm when he asked me to look at Moira's things . . .'

Anders patted her hand. 'I'm glad.'

They looked to the snowstorm, where the snow lay thick.

'How's Meg?' he asked softly.

How strange 'Meg' still sounded. She'd never heard her mother called anything other than 'Margaret' till she came to Shetland.

'She's well,' Lara replied with forced brightness.

He nodded, but the sadness remained.

'I thought you might have come for your grandmother's funeral.'

Lara felt the shame engulf her. First Magnus, now Anders . . . but with her grandfather there was no condemnation. He was simply stating a fact.

'Mum insisted on coming alone,' Lara answered slowly. 'Were you there?'

'Of course!' For a moment he didn't seem to be with her at all, then he smiled at her suddenly. 'I can't tell you how proud your grandmother would be to see you here.'

'Would you tell me about her?' Lara asked gently. She put his tea in front of him and sat beside him. She still wasn't sure if it was fair to bring all these memories and emotions back to him, especially when she herself couldn't comfort him — but she longed to know about her grandmother.

'What can I tell you?' Anders asked.

'Anything. I don't remember her at all. How did you meet?'

'We were at a dance in Lerwick . . . Moira was helping with the refreshments.'

Slowly, the sadness vanished, replaced by a roguish twinkle.

'She was the most beautiful girl I'd ever

seen. We danced together that evening, but she was careful to keep me at a distance. She was married to Iain, and I wasn't long over. The Bus was running — you know about the Bus? Every time we got to Norway it was harder to sail away again.'

Lara clasped his hand in hers.

'Even now, I don't know how it happened,' Anders went on. 'I used to seek Moira out in the end, and, whenever we were able, which wasn't often, we walked a lot and talked a lot. She was fiercely proud of Shetland and I was equally proud of Norway.' He smiled affectionately.

'We couldn't argue about that. She couldn't understand Norwegian and my English was very poor. It used to make her laugh. I picked up phrases here and there and then used them at inappropriate moments.'

Lara smiled. Every time her grandfather paused, she could tell he was reliving each conversation.

'I had to go to Norway. We were taking radio equipment and bringing back refugees. It was a couple of weeks before Christmas,' he remembered, 'and Moira made me promise to bring her back a Christmas present.'

Moira's way of making him promise to return safely . . .

'The snowstorm?' Lara guessed.

'Yes. We were delayed that trip. The Germans were searching for one of our intelligence men. There were Nazis everywhere, and we were forced into hiding before we could return to Shetland.'

Once again, he was reliving it all.

'A terrible storm blew up from nowhere. The wind settled into a furious roar. The boat was actually starting to break up.

'Not that I cared. I knew it would take more than a storm or a wreck to keep me from Moira.'

There was another long pause.

'And?' Lara prompted.

'We got back. Safe, but exhausted. The rest of the crew dropped into their beds, and I set off to see Moira. She lived miles from where we berthed, so I had to walk.'

'Was she waiting for you?' Lara asked, scarcely daring to breathe, but he didn't seem to hear her.

'It was early morning. She was walking her dog, and when she saw me, she raced across the field . . . ' He sighed.

'The Bus was supposed to be top secret, but everyone in the islands knew what was going on. They didn't know the details, though, so poor Moira hadn't known if I'd been drowned, shot or captured.' Those familiar blue-grey eyes shone. 'Tears of joy poured down her face . . .

'And so it was the end of January before Moira got her Christmas present.' Anders smiled at his granddaughter. 'We made such plans, Lara. After the war, we were going to marry, have a family, grow old together. Such simple plans.' That soft sigh again.

'We were young, and very much in love. As soon as the war ended — that's all we lived for, the end of that terrible war.

'But before then, your mother had been born. Iain had been home on leave and everyone assumed — ' His eyes hardened. 'We let them assume. 'As soon as the war ended', we said.

'But when the war ended, Iain came home . . . He was crippled, more emotionally than physically.'

His gaze rested on Lara for several moments.

'Moira wouldn't leave him.'

The air was heavy.

'Mum said she was twelve when Iain found out that she was your child? How did he find out, after so long?'

His eyes closed briefly.

'I told him.'

Lara gasped. 'You?'

'Yes,' Anders admitted with a sigh, 'and

your mother never forgave me.'

'But why? Why then? Why after twelve years?'

'Not to be with your child is — it's heartbreaking. I went back to Norway after the war, of course, and Moira sent me letters and photographs. When I came to Shetland, I'd see Meg for an hour or so.

'But it was hard, Lara. I longed for her to know who I was . . . '

His gaze was intense.

'The more years passed, the less I liked what I saw. Meg was quiet, withdrawn. I wanted her to be out, having fun, doing the things that children do . . . ' He sighed heavily.

'I'd just come back from Norway, and I went straight to the cottage. Moira was out. Iain had asked Meg to make him a drink, but something had distracted her and she'd forgotten. He didn't hear me arrive. He was shouting too loudly. Poor Meg fled in tears.'

Lara's own eyes filled with tears. Her mother had given her the happiest childhood possible . . . yet it seemed she'd never had that herself.

'Poor Iain,' Anders said with regret. 'It was his final humiliation. And poor Meg. Everything was so much worse after that. She blamed me, she blamed Moira. And she had every right to. She was robbed of her childhood.'

Lara kissed his cheek.

'Mum found her happiness,' she said urgently. 'She has a husband she loves, she's part of a big family. She's happy.'

She wished she could tell him that his little Meg had forgiven him . . .

Anders nodded. 'Yes. Your father is an exceptional man, Lara.'

'He is,' Lara agreed with feeling, 'but he couldn't heal the rift between my mother and Moira, could he?'

'Too much damage had been done. Do you remember coming to Shetland when you were four or five?'

Lara nodded.

'I'd flown over when I knew you would be here. I knew I was being selfish but I longed to see my grandchild. And Margaret, to her credit, let me take you for long walks. At least, you thought they were long!' His eyes twinkled.

'We searched for trows — Shetland's little people. We went beach-combing.

'Iain seemed — indifferent. And you — you were lovely, Lara. You were so inquisitive. You needed answers for everything.

'You wanted to know why Moira hadn't

married me instead of Iain, because, in your eyes, I was more fun. You wanted to know why I loved you more than Iain did . . .

'It was too much for Meg. She already blamed me for ruining her life. She said she wasn't going to let me ruin yours . . . And you never came back.'

His voice was hoarse as Lara lifted his hand and held it against her face.

'I'm back now.'

'Yes.'

'If only we could put back the clock,' she murmured.

'But we can't, Lara. If I could,' Anders said gruffly, 'I would have dragged Moira to the divorce courts, by force if necessary. But it was all different then.

'She'd promised before God to love, honour and obey Iain. When he came home from the war, needing her, she decided she had to do just that.'

'Was she very unhappy?' Lara asked quietly.

Anders gazed at her for a long time before he answered.

'I had my own business in Norway, but spent as much time as I could in Shetland. 'We have each other, Anders,' she used to say. 'Iain has no one.' And, in a way, she was right. Despite the miles that separated us most of the time, we were closer than many couples are.'

Gently, Lara lifted his cup, and he smiled before he sipped the tea.

'A few years after Iain died, Moira agreed to visit Norway for the first time. She said then that although we hadn't realised our dreams, we'd been luckier than most. We'd been through it all together.' Once more, his gaze was drawn to the snowstorm.

'Every time she saw me, Lara, her face shone with happiness. At those times, it would have been impossible to say that she wasn't happy. It was that face, that smile, that I carried with me. Whenever I crossed the sea, during the war and through all the years that followed, I saw that smile.'

Silence settled around them.

'I see it now,' Anders said softly.

* * *

Lara gazed at the water below her and wished that she could be anywhere but on the *Shearwater*.

It had been Anders' suggestion. Anders, who yearned for the sea, wanted Lara to see Lunna, home of the Shetland Bus before the operation had moved to Scalloway.

Magnus was concerned that the trip might

124

be too much for Anders, but he was always keen to take the *Shearwater* out and in the end, he'd agreed.

Fran, too, was more than happy to take a pleasure trip on the last day of her holiday. Although she would have been much happier, Lara guessed, if she could have been with Alisdair. Fran's 'short' holiday in Shetland had stretched to two-and-a-half weeks and it was Alisdair who had made her forget her first love, her business, *Shoestring*.

Alisdair, though, was moving sheep. Apparently, he owed a friend a favour and it was time to return it.

So Lara was trying to look as if she was enjoying every moment, and hoping that no one would look too closely at her green, sickly complexion . . .

Magnus had looked closely. He was well aware she didn't like boats, but he'd thought no one could fail to enjoy a short trip on his precious boat, especially when conditions were so perfect. He was clearly wrong; Lara looked ill.

She was doing it for Anders, and Magnus admired her for it.

It was Shona who'd changed his mind about the trip, about Lara spending so much time with Anders.

'Think of your dad, Magnus,' Shona had

said. 'Anders came to mean everything to you, but he could never replace your dad, could he?

'It's the same with Lara. No one can change what you and Anders have but, like it or not, Lara will give him more happiness than we ever could.'

She was right, of course. One glance at the two of them together was enough to tell Magnus that.

He'd half-expected some kind of explanation from Anders, but he should have known better.

'So what do you think of my granddaughter, Magnus?' Anders had said, brows beetling.

Magnus had replied with an evasive, 'You must be very proud of her.'

And that, Magnus thought now, had to be the biggest understatement of his life.

Anders just laughed. 'Very diplomatic!'

* * *

As Magnus took the *Shearwater* into Lunna Voe, Anders insisted on being by his side, to see it as he'd seen it so many times before. Lara and Fran followed him, leaving them little room to breathe, let alone move.

'This, I think, is God's own country,'

Anders said. 'It was perfect for the Bus. So remote. Sheltered from the wind in every direction. There was just the house — big enough to be crammed full of men — the farm, the manse and — ' he pointed ' — the kirk.'

'And no one knew you were here?' Fran marvelled.

Anders smiled. 'We thought no one in Shetland could possibly know what was going on, but they did. They never said anything, but they knew. For the most part though, no one saw the boats sail and no one saw them return.'

He seemed to lose himself in memories.

'I cannot describe the joy, the relief or the sense of triumph as we sailed into this little bay.'

Lara linked her arm through his. 'And yet it was so far from home.'

He shook his head sadly.

'No — not home. Norway had been neutral during the first war, and she'd intended to remain that way. There was no warning, no declaration of war. But suddenly our buildings were displaying the swastika. Our streets echoed with the sound of jackboots. People stood in the streets and wept.

'No. Until we had won Norway's freedom back, we had no home there.'

The four of them looked towards Lunna House, temporary home of those Norwegian sailors. Lara tightened her grip on her grandfather's arm.

'I've been thinking about Jakob,' Anders said quietly.

'Your brother?' Magnus was wary.

'I did see him before we sailed from Solund. I know I did. And he was worried. He knew something. He knew, somehow, that he wouldn't make it to Shetland that trip.'

'Anders,' Magnus said gently, 'when you last spoke of Jakob, you weren't sure if you'd seen him, or if you'd imagined it, or if — '

'Now I'm sure!' Anders interrupted firmly. 'He'd brought lots of treasures out of Norway,' Anders went on with a frown, 'saving them from enemy hands. I think he was bringing — ' He paused.

'In Norway, we had a shield, a great symbol called the Kristiansund Jewel. Some said it belonged to King Harald. Others believed it was Eystein Haraldsson's or Eystein Magnusson's. Anyway, legend had it that if ever the shield was lost, Norway would be lost, too.'

'And you think your brother was bringing that to Shetland?' Magnus asked quietly.

Anders nodded. 'For safekeeping.'

'And you think he knew he wouldn't make it. How?'

128

'Perhaps he had a premonition,' Anders said impatiently. 'Perhaps he heard something . . . the place was crawling with Nazis.'

'Surely, anything he was bringing back, would have been lost with him?'

'Possibly, but Jakob was — ' Anders smiled. 'He was like you, Magnus. He was fascinated by the history of our land. While we were busy running in special operations men, he was risking his neck for Norway's treasures. No, he might have risked his life, but he would never have risked our country's heritage . . .

'He wouldn't have taken the Kristiansund Jewel on a trip he knew was doomed. Yet since the war, it's never been seen.'

'Are any of Jakob's crew still alive?' Lara asked.

Anders' eyes gleamed with a sudden spark.

'That's an idea. I've been chasing round the museums to see what I can find out but . . . the last I heard, Hugo was still alive. I'll get in touch with him and see what he can remember.'

Magnus wished he would forget all about it. In his opinion, worrying about the existence or otherwise of some Viking artefact was the last thing Anders needed.

'We'd better make our way back . . . ' was all he said.

Lara was feeling better. Whether it was because her stomach had adjusted to the rocking movement of the *Shearwater*, whether it was because sitting on deck chatting to Fran and Anders had taken her mind off it, or whether it was the promise of soon being on dry land, she wasn't sure.

The sudden, violent lurch as the *Shearwater* changed direction and crashed over its own wash, took her completely by surprise.

'What the — '

Anders was on his feet. His expression frightened Lara.

Magnus was on the two-way radio. The boat was speeding up, but he seemed calm enough.

He must have known they were waiting for some explanation but it was a long time coming. 'The *Celia* has put out a distress call. She's taking in water.'

'Dear God!' Anders breathed, his voice a rasping whisper.

'The *Celia*,' Fran cried. 'But Ally's on that!'

'Fran!' Lara said in amazement. 'He's moving sheep!'

'Yes, they're taking them off the island.' Fran knocked Lara aside, grabbed Magnus, and tugged on his arm. 'What do they mean? What does taking in water mean? He's going to drown, isn't he?'

Lara saw all this as if it were happening in slow motion. Nothing seemed to register.

'No, he isn't. Don't be ridiculous. And let me get on with my job.' He shook off her hand, and Fran burst into tears.

Lara grabbed her arm. 'Calm down, Fran! The boat's taking in water, that's all. It doesn't follow that it'll sink, but if it does, they'll abandon it. They'll have a life-raft, life-jackets.'

She was appalled at Fran's selfishness. After all, Alisdair was Magnus' brother.

'We can't do anything to help Magnus,' Anders told Fran with a firmness that surprised Lara. He took hold of Fran's arm and said, 'We'll keep an eye out on deck while these two stay here, shall we?'

Fran, still in tears, allowed herself to be led away.

Lara stood beside Magnus, feeling sick and swaying on her feet as she tried to adjust to the corkscrew motion of the *Shearwater*. Magnus, hands on the wheel, looking ahead, was completely still.

'Sorry about Fran,' she said quietly. 'She's not very good in a crisis.'

'So I noticed,' he replied grimly.

'*Is* the boat likely to sink?' she asked anxiously.

'Yes.'

'But they'll have life-jackets, won't they?'

'Yes. If they have time to put them on.'

The radio wasn't silent for a moment but Lara didn't catch a word of what was being said. It reminded her of the surgery. It never failed to amaze her that, having called a patient through, that patient actually heard their name over the speaker and arrived.

Then she heard every word of the coastguard's appeal for assistance from any vessels in the area. The *Celia* was sinking.

She was too shocked to utter a word. It seemed so unreal. The sun was shining . . .

Magnus glanced at her briefly. 'We're not too far away, and this is a good, fast boat.'

Lara couldn't say a word. She wasn't even sure if he was talking to her, or to himself.

'We lost a boat about nine years ago,' Magnus remarked after a while. His eyes were scanning the horizon now. 'We were about six miles from land when she started taking in water. It was three in the morning and I was asleep.

'Jim Cook was in the wheelhouse and when he came to wake me, she was already listing to the port side. We woke Ally and Ivan, but by then, she was over on her side.

'It happened so fast. I put out a quick mayday but there was no time to put on proper clothes or life-jackets. We had to climb out of the wheelhouse and along the mast — it was lying in water by then — to get to the liferaft. We seemed to be in the water an age before we could upturn that liferaft.'

Lara didn't want to hear the story but she knew he was talking to take his mind off the *Celia*. Besides, if he kept talking, it might take *her* mind off Shona.

'Take my glasses, would you?' He nodded at a pair of powerful binoculars. 'Sweep over there to the right. That's where she is . . .

'We set off a couple of distress flares but we weren't hopeful. We were lucky, though. The coastguard had picked up our mayday and the lifeboat was launched.'

Lara couldn't even begin to imagine what that must be like. Her mind refused to picture it, it was too awful.

'You must have been terrified.'

'Not at the time,' he replied thoughtfully. 'Even at times like that, I suppose the skipper has to at least look as if everything's under control. But afterwards — yes, it was quite a while before I slept easy.'

'And yet you still spend half your life at sea!'

'It's what I am,' Magnus said simply.

That logic, if there was any logic there, was completely lost on Lara.

People laughed at her fear of boats. Anders

and Magnus spoke of the sea as if it were a kindly, benevolent mistress. All Lara saw was a heaving, black mass of angry water. She looked at it now, tossing spitefully around the *Shearwater*, quite capable of smashing the boat to pieces.

She could only admire the courage of the man beside her — or possibly his obstinacy. She was sure that was what his mother would call it.

Sweeping the binoculars round in an arc, she frowned suddenly. Had that been a speck on the water? She adjusted the focusing.

'Magnus — over there!'

He turned the boat in the direction she was pointing, and grabbed the binoculars, putting her hands on the wheel.

'Just keep her straight . . . Oh, Lara, you're right. It's the raft . . . '

Minutes later, five men, including Alisdair, were aboard the *Shearwater*. They were wet, cold, and very shaken, but, miraculously, they were safe.

Despite their protests, Lara examined each one of them. They were well, wanting only to go home and dry off.

Luckily, they'd already landed the sheep when the *Celia* began taking in water, and Magnus could head for home.

In fact, when they all traded the deck of the

134

Shearwater for dry land, it was Fran who was in the worst shape. Lara had been keeping an eye on her grandfather, who was exhausted, but Fran looked terrible. Even Alisdair's arm round her hadn't banished the fear from her eyes.

★ ★ ★

After tea that evening, Lara walked with Tony to his car. He was due at a meeting in Lerwick, leaving Lara with Fran and Alisdair.

'I'll see you tomorrow, darling. About eight?'

Lara nodded.

'Who knows,' he added dryly, 'we might even manage a few moments alone!'

'I hope so. It has to be said that for someone who's visiting me, Fran's spending a lot of time with Alisdair!'

Tony bent his head to kiss her.

'I'll be on call,' she reminded him, 'so we won't be able to go far.'

'Then let's hope everyone stays nice and healthy, because I've been trying to talk to you for days.'

'What about?' she asked curiously.

A Land Rover roared along the road and pulled up by the verge. Magnus waved as he

135

switched off the engine.

'It's worse than Piccadilly in the rush hour,' Tony muttered.

'What did you want to talk to me about?' Lara persisted.

'It'll keep.' He cupped her face in his hands. 'I'll see you tomorrow.'

His kiss was — well, it was just a kiss. She had no need to feel embarrassed but, as she looked at Magnus, who was staring intently at his feet, she did.

'Sorry, can't stop, Magnus,' Tony said briskly. 'I'm late for a meeting.'

Lara watched him drive away, and then turned back to Magnus. 'Are you coming in?'

He looked towards where Alisdair's car was parked. 'No, thanks. I just came over to — well, about today. I know you don't like boats and I'm sorry about — If I'd known how things were going to turn out — '

Shona was right, Lara thought. Magnus *should* have been born with webbed feet. At sea, he was totally at ease, in any situation, but now he was struggling to put a sentence together.

'And I wanted to say thanks,' he got out at last.

'For what?' Lara asked in amazement.

'For listening. For keeping me company. For being there.'

The simple, unexpected words touched her deeply. There was a frankness in his expression that made him look very vulnerable. It was impossible to equate him with the man who usually kept his feelings so well hidden.

'Magnus, can we go somewhere and talk?'

'Yes, of course.'

'Let me get a jacket.'

Lara ran inside, went up the stairs to get her jacket and called to Fran and Alisdair on her way out. 'I'm just going with Magnus. I won't be long.'

She'd expected to walk but Magnus was back in the driving seat, and his passenger door was open.

'I hate all these quarrels between us, Magnus,' she said as he drove them away from the house.

'There aren't any quarrels between us,' he answered quietly. 'A few ghosts maybe, but no quarrels. Not any more.'

He stopped a couple of miles from the house, close to the shore. They got out and walked along the beach. The shingle crunched beneath their feet.

'Could you survive out of sight of the sea?' Lara asked with amusement.

Magnus thought about it. 'If I had to.' Then realisation dawned. 'You'd rather go somewhere else? We can go for a coffee, or something to eat.'

She laughed. 'No, it's nice here. Really.'

Things had changed between them, she knew that. But the ghosts were still there.

'Magnus, I'm not making excuses,' she began carefully, 'but I want to explain things . . .'

Slowly, she told him the whole story. She left nothing out, from the moment she had applied for the post in Shetland. She described the shock of her mother's revelations, the bitter-sweet experience of finding her grandfather, the love she had for Anders.

He didn't interrupt once.

Once she'd poured it all out, they walked in silence for a while. He was thinking and, when he spoke, typically, his concern was for the present, not the past.

'You have to talk to your mother,' he said. 'You know how ill Anders is. There isn't much time.'

'I've tried,' Lara said. 'I speak to her often, but it's so hard to tell her over the phone. I even spent three hours writing a letter but, on my way to post it, I imagined her opening it. I tore it up.

'But it's not just the telling her,' she explained. 'I want her here. I want her to see her father. I want her to come here ready to forget, and more importantly, to forgive. And I want that for her sake, as much as for Anders'.'

She sighed heavily. 'I want a lot, don't I? But I can't bear any more of this awful — waste.'

As their feet crunched along the shingle, a group of oystercatchers flew off in a flash of black and white, peeping their annoyance.

'We met, you know,' Magnus remarked, 'when you came to see Moira that last time.'

Lara felt again the pull of those invisible ties that bound her to this place. 'Did we?'

'Yes. I'd forgotten until Mum reminded me. Ally and I had called on Moira — I expect the fact that you were staying had pushed our noses out of joint.

'The grown-ups wanted to talk, so yours truly was entrusted with the precious Lara. I wasn't to take you out of sight of the cottage, or within ten yards of the water, and I wasn't — under any circumstances whatsoever — to let go of your hand.' Magnus smiled at the memory.

'We'd been gone less than five minutes when I found a dead gannet. When I picked it up to show it to you, you screamed like I have never heard anyone scream before.

'You ran off and, as I was chasing after you, you fell over. When the grown-ups arrived, all you could do was scream as you showed them your grazed hands and knees. My name was mud!

'And your mother was furious. She thought it was Moira's fault for letting you go off with those wild Cameron boys.' He paused for a moment. 'A childhood spent in London is very different to one spent here. Compared to you, I expect we did seem a bit wild.'

'Poor Granny,' Lara said wistfully.

Unless they wanted to scramble over rocks, and Lara didn't, they could walk no further.

'Friends?' she asked softly.

Magnus reached for her hand and gave it a gentle squeeze. 'Of course.'

They turned around and started walking back.

The sun was setting. The oystercatchers had returned to their spot and, making even more noise than before, they flew off again.

Magnus was still holding her hand. She could easily have changed that, simply by stopping to pick up a shell or a pebble, but she didn't want to. Their shoulders touched as they walked.

Magnus made life seem so simple and, as they walked, Lara knew a deep contentment, a certain knowledge that everything would work out for the best . . .

When he stopped the Land Rover outside

Little Bay, Alisdair's car was still there.

'I'm surprised your brother hasn't moved in at my place. Fran was only intending to stay for a week!'

Magnus smiled. 'Alisdair and his women . . .'

They got out of the Land Rover.

'Are you coming in?' Lara asked.

'Better not. I've got an early start in the morning and a million things to do before then.'

Lara frowned, puzzled. 'But I thought Alisdair said the *Ermingerd* wasn't going out until Tuesday.'

'She isn't. But I'm not going with them. I'm going down to Buckie tomorrow with Ivan.'

'How long will you be gone?'

'A week. Ten days perhaps. Ivan's bought a new boat but it needs a small repair job.'

He gazed at her hands, and Lara was surprised to realise that they were trembling.

'I'm truly sorry about today, Lara.'

The tenderness in his voice made her tremble all the more.

'I was fine. Really.'

He reached out for her hands, and turned them over in his. They were small, pale and soft by comparison.

'You were quite safe, you know,' he said

gently. 'I wouldn't have let anything happen to you.'

'I know. I felt safe.' Lara's voice was suddenly hoarse.

She had known that, sooner or later, this would happen. Part of her had even wanted it to happen. But now, as he pulled her gently into his arms, and as she felt the warmth of his lips on hers, she could almost hear Shona's words.

Lara could feel his heart thumping against hers. Or perhaps it was her own. Or perhaps their hearts were beating as one.

And still she could hear the pain in his mother's voice as she'd talked about his father.

worshipped every step he took . . . thought there was nothing he couldn't do . . . my husband . . . father of my children . . . my best friend . . . my hero . . . when you lose your hero, life's never quite the same again . . .

And here was Robbie's son, making Lara feel exactly the same. She longed to stay in the safe circle of his arms. But even as her fingers dug into his shoulders, even as those fingers lost themselves in his hair, Lara remembered how Shona's dreams had crumbled to nothing . . .

6

Driving home through rain that hadn't stopped all day, Lara wondered again what it was that Tony wanted to discuss with her.

For various reasons, they saw less of each other these days but it was obvious that he was happier, and far more relaxed. Not just happier, but happy.

Perhaps he'd finally let go of the past? Perhaps he was ready to face the future? If he asked her to marry him, what would she say?

It was what she had wanted for years so she would say yes. Of course she would.

Yet last night, when Magnus had left, he'd touched her face, said, 'I'll see you when I get back,' then he had kissed her again.

Lara could still feel the warmth of his touch, could still feel his lips on hers. He'd been with her all day, stubbornly refusing to leave her thoughts for a moment.

But when he came back, it would be as if nothing had happened between them. It would *have* to be. Emotions had been running high. They would chalk it down to the heat of the moment . . .

Once home, she had a long, hot shower,

and wandered around aimlessly, making a mental note of chores that needed doing, watching the rain, and wondering what possessed men to go to sea . . .

In an hour or so, she might be engaged — and she had never felt more depressed in her life.

She picked up the phone and tapped out her parents' number. Her mother answered almost immediately.

'Lara! What a lovely surprise. I was going to ring you later. Your dad's working late . . . '

As Margaret gave her all the news, Lara knew a sudden longing for London. Or if not London, then her mother's sitting room.

'You're very quiet,' her mother noticed. 'Everything all right?'

'Fine,' Lara replied automatically. She told her mother what they'd been doing, how Fran was enjoying her visit and, without mentioning Anders, she told her about their trip on the *Shearwater* the previous day.

'You're getting very friendly with the Camerons.' her mother remarked. 'I always liked Shona, but those boys — they were real tearaways. Not boys now, of course.'

'Alisdair's the same age as me,' Lara reminded her.

'Yes. And Magnus would be — what? — five years older? When we visited Shetland that last time, I remember he frightened you half to death with an enormous dead bird.'

'A gannet,' Lara said softly.

'I expect he's changed a lot. From what I heard, he took his father's death very badly. But who wouldn't? A tragedy like that rocks the whole community. Not that I've seen much of him, of course. I saw him at Iain's funeral and then at my mother's. He read the twenty-third Psalm. He and Alisdair were among those carrying the coffin . . .'

Lara's eyes filled with tears. She could picture it so clearly. The rain and wind at the graveyard by the shore, Magnus saying a final farewell to his dear friend, her mother coping with all the regrets. And Anders . . .

'Lara?' Her mother's shocked voice penetrated the silence. 'Darling, you're crying!'

Lara reached for a tissue. She didn't know why she was crying . . . for Moira, for Anders, or for her mother . . .

'Mum, I need to talk to you,' she gulped out.

'Then talk, darling,' her mother urged her. 'You can always talk to us, you know that. That's what we're here for. We told you, if you're not happy, then you must come straight home . . .'

'I am happy,' Lara assured her, brushing the tears away.

'Then what — '

'We need to talk, Mum. You and I. About your father.'

The silence was awful.

'You've seen him?'

'Yes.'

Again, that awful silence.

'He's not well, Mum.'

'I assumed he was in Norway.' Margaret's voice was cold. She might never have heard what Lara said.

'No, he's come home.'

Home. For Anders, home should have been Norway. But it wasn't. Home was where his friends were, home was where his memories were, home was where he could put white chrysanthemums on a grave . . .

'Anders is dying, Mum,' Lara said bluntly. 'It's lung cancer, and he doesn't have long. I've been trying to spend time with him — though it's not easy. George really did need a partner — we both work long hours.'

Still that silence at the other end.

'He talks about you, Mum,' Lara said softly. 'About how hard it was for him to be parted from you — especially when you didn't know the truth . . . '

There was a sound from the other end of the line.

'Mum?'

'How long is — not long?' Margaret asked.

'Months perhaps. Not very many months. I wish I could tell you different. I'm going to miss him so much, Mum.'

'We'll come and see you,' Margaret announced suddenly.

'Oh, Mum. Would you? It would mean so much to me.'

'We can't come this week,' Margaret said, her voice shaking. 'But next week — I'll have a word with your dad when he gets home. I suppose I could come on my own but I'd rather . . .'

'I know,' Lara replied, understanding. She too would rather her father came.

'I'll speak to him,' Margaret promised, 'and tomorrow, I'll organise the tickets. Meanwhile, don't let it upset you, darling. I'll give you a ring in the morning, Lara. Just to make sure you're all right. I hate to think of you stuck up there on your own . . .'

When the call ended, Lara felt much better. She'd despaired of ever seeing her mother on Shetland soil. Letters and phone calls were all well and good, but they weren't the same.

Tony's car pulled up outside just then.

Shetland was good for him, Lara thought. He looked fit, and happy — just as he had when she'd first met him. So handsome, too. Part of his charm was the way he was

147

completely unaware of it. Always thoughtful, always kind and caring. Never, in all the years she'd known him, had she heard him utter a bad word about anyone.

They made and ate a meal together, moving round each other with the familiar ease born of long friendship. It wasn't till they were sitting over coffee that Lara brought up the subject.

'You wanted to talk to me?'

'Oh, that's right. About Anna Thompson.'

Lara stared at him. 'Anna Thompson? You want to talk about a patient?'

She didn't know whether to laugh or cry. She'd imagined a proposal of marriage. She had even imagined that she would say yes.

But deep down, she'd known. How could she have said yes when she'd spent the entire day thinking of another man? When she was thinking of him even now?

'Anna called me,' Tony was explaining. 'She said you were sending her to see James Bartholomew.'

'That's right.' Lara nodded.

'Lara, it's frightening her to death. You know how people feel about counselling.'

'Yes, but they're wrong.'

'But so long as they're thinking that way, what good can it do? Surely there's something more practical . . . '

'I could always pump her full of chemicals,' Lara retorted. 'Would you prefer that?'

'At least that way she wouldn't be convinced she was going mad! She needs — '

'Anna needs love,' Lara cut him off. 'When we hit rock bottom, that's what we all need. Most of us are lucky, we have family and friends. But Anna has no one, except her little girl. And until she gets her confidence back, she won't have anyone.

'James gets good results,' she went on. 'She might need medication as well, but she might not. I'd rather we tried the counselling first.'

'I think you're wrong,' Tony said levelly.

'Right or wrong, she's my patient! This has nothing whatsoever to do with you, Tony!'

'OK. Forget I mentioned it.'

That was impossible. The evening was ruined. Not that it had stood much of a chance, Lara thought ruefully. She'd been on edge all day. And there was one thing she had to say to him.

'I think,' she said, when Tony was leaving, 'that we ought to stop seeing quite so much of each other.'

He stared back at her as if she were speaking a foreign language.

'I seem to be trying to fit too much into a day,' she explained quickly. 'What with seeing Anders, getting involved with this and that. I need — I need some time to myself, Tony.'

'Mm.' He brushed her hair out of her eyes with a gentle hand. 'About Anna — I wasn't criticising, Lara.'

'I know. This has nothing to do with Anna. Everything seems upside down at the moment, that's all. Mum and Dad will be up next week — I just need some time, Tony. I'll call you. OK?'

He looked at her for a long time.

'If that's you want.'

* * *

Shona Cameron clutched at the back of a kitchen chair as pain shot through her side. She sank on to the chair and put her head down, waiting for the pain to subside and for her head to clear.

It would pass in a minute, it always did. But while it lasted . . .

She groaned as she heard someone knocking on the door. Then she remembered. Lara had said she would call in on her way home from the surgery.

She sat up, and forced a smile to her face. 'It's open!'

'Are you all right, Shona?' Lara asked curiously.

'Fine,' she lied, 'I'm just getting my breath

150

back. I've been moving furniture around.'

Lara's searching gaze took in everything. A doctor's look, Shona thought grimly. But the pain had subsided to a dull ache and Shona was able to smile more easily.

'I was waiting for an excuse to put the kettle on.'

'I'll do it,' Lara offered immediately.

Shona watched her, seeing the same restless movements that had puzzled her when she'd called on Lara earlier in the week. Her fingers refused to be still, drumming on the worktop as she waited for the kettle to boil.

Something was troubling her, that much was obvious.

'Are your parents packed?' Perhaps it was their visit that was worrying her.

'Yes, they'll be here on Friday.'

Shona was relieved. If any girl looked as if she needed her mother, it was Lara.

'How's Tony?' she asked. 'I haven't seen much of him lately?'

'Fine.' Lara glanced at her. 'Actually, we've agreed to see less of each other. Oh, we haven't had a row or anything, but, well, I seem to be getting roped into a hundred-and-one different things, and our hours don't coincide . . . '

Shona wondered exactly what had gone

wrong. She didn't imagine it had anything to do with the feeble excuses Lara had trotted out.

Lara didn't have sugar in her tea but for all that she was intent on stirring the bottom of the cup away.

'Have you heard from Magnus?'

Shona wasn't sure which surprised her most, the question or the unnatural voice in which it was asked.

'Magnus? No. But I wouldn't expect to.'

Lara's fingers refused to be still.

'What's bothering you, lass?' Shona probed gently.

'Nothing.' Her smile was overbright.

Shona raised her eyebrows.

'Well, there's Mum and Dad's visit. Tongues have been wagging a bit lately and Mum's going to hate that. I don't know if she'll even see Anders — I have visions of her not leaving the house.'

'You must bring them here,' Shona offered immediately. 'How about Saturday night? I haven't seen your mother for years, except at funerals — or your dad. It'll be fine. I expect Alisdair will be around. Magnus, too. I'll do a long-drawn-out meal so that everyone will be too busy eating to notice any awkward pauses.'

'Shona, you're a gem.' Lara touched

her arm. 'Thank you.'

Shona's pain had completely gone, as if it had never been, which proved that it was nothing worth worrying about. So why couldn't she stop worrying about it?

She got up to put a selection of home-made biscuits on a plate.

'He's like his father, isn't he?'

'Sorry, love?' Shona turned around.

A wave of pink crept into Lara's cheeks.

'Magnus. I was just thinking — I wondered if he was like his father.'

Shona glanced sharply at her, but Lara's head was bent.

'In a lot of ways he is, although his dad was more happy-go-lucky. Less of a perfectionist.'

'It must have been hard, bringing up two boys on your own,' Lara murmured.

'Not hard exactly, but it was worrying, especially at first. Alisdair wasn't too bad. He cried a lot, he had terrible dreams, he became very clingy, but I could cope with that. A hug, a chat, a bit of reassurance and all would be well until the next time.

'But Magnus — of course, he was five years older. Fourteen's a difficult age, no longer a child and a long way from being a man. He did cry, I saw his red, swollen eyes, but he never cried in front of me. If I tried to reassure him, he'd put his arm round me and say, 'We'll be all right, Mum.' '

Lara seemed paler than ever. Shona was about to change the subject when Lara asked, 'Did he like school?'

'Some of it,' Shona replied, 'but not a lot. He was obsessed with navigation and, of course, that was never on the curriculum. As soon as he left school, he went to Aberdeen to study that.'

Lara helped herself to a biscuit.

'What about girlfriends?'

All these questions were making Shona uneasy. She would have put it down to a natural interest if any of the questions had included Alisdair.

'There's been no one he was serious about. Except Jess perhaps.'

'Jess?' Lara had never heard of Jess.

'She moved here from Cornwall.' Shona was smiling. 'What you'd call a free spirit, I suppose. That would be ten years ago now. Magnus had just got the *Shearwater* and I remember she used to take that boat out without telling him — few folk could get away with that!'

'On her own?' Lara was shocked. Obviously Jess didn't share her own dread of the sea.

'I expect that was part of the attraction. Magnus finally found someone who was as passionate about the sea as he is!'

Lara stared into her cup. 'What happened?'

'I never really knew,' Shona admitted. 'She left Shetland and that was the end of it.'

Lara drank her tea, leaving Shona wondering. Obviously Lara wasn't as indifferent to Magnus as his mother had thought. Or — with things going badly between her and Tony . . . had Lara recognised how Magnus felt about her? Could she be using him to get back at Tony?

At once, Shona dismissed the unkind thought. Lara wouldn't use anyone, not consciously, at any rate.

Perhaps she really did feel something for Magnus? They say that opposites attract. But no, they went beyond opposites. Lara and her elder son existed in totally different worlds . . .

* * *

Magnus spotted Lara standing at the water's edge. Her hands were thrust into the pockets of her skirt and she was staring at the water. She was completely still, and he could have watched her for hours.

Despite what his imagination had conjured up during the last eight days, he was wishing for the moon, and he knew it.

The feel of her fingers linked through his as they'd walked along the beach, the softness of her kiss . . . She'd dismiss it all, he was sure. She would blame the loss of the *Celia* for playing havoc with her emotions that evening. She would remind him about Tony . . .

Lara lifted her hand to brush a strand of hair from her face, and he walked towards her. His feet crunched on the pebbles, and he was only a couple of yards from her when she turned around.

'Magnus!' A sudden smile sparkled in her eyes. 'How long have you been back?'

'About an hour.'

She reached for his hands, and held them tightly in her own. After what seemed an age, she said, 'It is so good to have you home.'

He could feel his heart hammering in his throat as he pulled her into his arms, and her soft sigh was lost on the breeze as he kissed her. The feelings he'd relived over and over during the last eight days came flooding back. He felt as if he'd spent his entire life waiting for her . . .

But when he finally drew away and looked into her face, he saw tears shimmering in her eyes. He traced a finger around the dark circles surrounding those eyes.

'What's happened, Lara?'

'I've missed you,' she replied shakily.

'I've missed you, too.'

She gazed at him. 'It's all happening so fast, Magnus. It's frightening.'

'No,' he argued gently. 'How can it be frightening?'

'There's no future in it.' His heart contracted.

'It's so — senseless. I can't get involved with you, Magnus. I'm a doctor. I can't allow anything to intrude on my work.'

'I — I don't understand.' Magnus stared back at her blankly.

'It's what you do,' she told him urgently. 'Every drop of rain — every time I've heard the wind — I've even been listening to the shipping forecasts. I hate it. I hate looking at the sea and knowing that someone I — someone I know is out there.'

'Lara, this is ridiculous. You can't — '

'And that's what I hate more than anything! You dismiss the dangers. Anders is the same. You have this 'it'll never happen to me' view of life. It's all a game.'

'No,' he said. 'There are dangers, of course there are. But there are dangers in anything. You can get killed crossing the road. It's a job, Lara. Just like any other.'

'I know,' she admitted helplessly. 'But just look at your mum, Magnus. I saw her on

Friday, and she looked — well, almost ill. Tired. Old.'

'She does worry,' Magnus answered carefully, 'and she seems worse than ever lately. But I think there's something else worrying her. She says there isn't, of course, but — '

Lara shook her head.

'Don't you think years of worrying are beginning to take their toll? What has the sea ever done for her?'

Magnus hugged her close. 'But even if she'd known what would happen to Dad, she wouldn't have had it any differently. She would still have married him. And Dad loved what he did. He loved the sea, the wind, the rain, the sun, the space, the freedom . . . '

'Just as you do?'

'Yes.'

'And if there's a price to pay?'

'Then you have to pay it.'

Lara shivered in his arms.

Magnus was at a complete and utter loss. He simply hadn't expected this.

He slipped his arm around her shoulders. 'You're cold. Are you doing anything tonight?'

She shook her head.

'You're not seeing Tony?' he asked, trying to sound casual, and she smiled.

'No. I told him I thought it was best if we

didn't see so much of each other, Magnus.'
She gazed up at him. 'I've never felt like this
before.'

'Neither have I.' Magnus touched her face.

She smiled, a real smile that almost hid the
dark smudges round her eyes and Magnus
hugged her again.

'Let's go into town and get something to
eat. I haven't eaten for hours.'

Her arm went around his waist as they
walked, and her head touched his shoulder.
He should have been walking on air but he
wasn't. The pebbles were firm beneath his
feet and he felt as if he was walking on
eggshells. One false move, one wrong word
and he could lose her. Because he wouldn't,
couldn't give up the sea . . .

He wondered what the coming winter had
in store. How would Lara cope with the
savage storms that the islanders took for
granted, and the days when it was too
dangerous for the ferries to operate.

'Your mum told me about Jess.' Lara
looked up at him.

'Jess? Good grief. Whatever made her think
about Jess? That's ancient history.'

'I asked her.'

'I see.' Magnus smiled.

'Did you love her?'

'No.'

'Did she love you?'

Magnus considered this for a moment.

'She thought she did.'

'Perhaps she did.' Lara looked up at him.

'Perhaps,' he said lightly.

'What was she like?'

'She came from Cornwall. Her mother had remarried, leaving her and her five brothers with her father. He was a fisherman, and her brothers, too.

'Jess wanted a change, so she came to Shetland. She loved it for a while. We had fun together. We'd been seeing each other for a month, maybe two, when she decided it would be a good idea if we got married.

'Marriage was the last thing on my mind. And in any case, Jess wasn't the type anyone married. She was too busy trying to find just what she wanted from life.

'When she left here, she went to live in France. I had one postcard from her, and she thought she'd found paradise. Six months later, I had a Christmas card. She was back in Cornwall.'

'Is she still there?'

'I don't know. I haven't heard from her since.' He watched her face as they walked along, and added gently, 'It didn't mean a lot, Lara. Not even at the time.'

'I can see that.' Lara changed the subject.

'Magnus, my parents are arriving the day after tomorrow.'

'Oh? How long are they staying?'

'Two weeks.' Before he could say anything, she added, 'Your mum's an angel, she's invited us to dinner on Saturday night. I think she feels sorry for any visitors I have.'

'I'm not surprised,' Magnus retorted. 'According to Ally, he had to save your last guest from starvation. And Fran says the most complex thing you manage is opening a packet.'

'I didn't see it as a mercy mission.' Lara said, laughing. 'He couldn't keep away from her!'

'Like I can't keep away from you?'

Lara's kiss was his answer.

★ ★ ★

On Thursday, Tony was leaving the hospital for the day when he spotted Anna Thompson in the car park, struggling to unlock the door of her car.

'Hello, Anna.'

At the sound of his voice, the keys flew from her hands.

Tony stooped to pick them up. 'Sorry, I didn't mean to startle you.'

'No, I know.' She took the keys from him.

'Sorry, I'm a bit jumpy.'

Tony knew she'd been for her first appointment with James Bartholomew. 'How did it go?' he asked.

'It wasn't as bad as I expected.'

'It never is.' Tony smiled.

She fumbled with her car keys again.

'Look, would you like to come for a coffee?'

Her face flushed with colour. 'Oh, no. Thanks, but no. I mean, it's very kind of you but there's no need . . . '

'I know there isn't, but I'd like some coffee so you'd be doing me a favour.'

'OK. Thanks.' She gave him a shy smile.

They went back in to the hospital and, on the short walk, Tony wondered why he'd asked her. He'd planned to drive straight home.

When their coffees were sitting in front of them, she told him what James had said.

'I've got to see him every week, which is what I expected. Doctor Daniels thought he'd say that. She's marvellous, you know. She has endless time and patience. She's even given me her home telephone number, and said I can call her anytime.'

'Lara's one of the best. She has a knack of putting herself in other people's shoes and knowing just how they feel. I know, I speak from experience.'

Anna looked at him, curiously.

'I was married. Jane, my wife — There was an accident and she was killed.'

'Tony, no! I'm so sorry, I had no idea.'

It was the first time she'd called him Tony, he realised. At first it had been Doctor Adams but since he'd pointed out that he wasn't her doctor, or her grandfather's doctor, and that his name was Tony, she hadn't called him anything.

'What I'm trying to say is that Lara helped me through that.'

'I'm sorry,' she said again.

'It wasn't the best of marriages,' he admitted. 'I loved Jane, I couldn't have loved her more, but — perhaps a marriage needs more than love. I don't know.'

He had never said that to anyone, not even to Lara. Quite the reverse in fact. To Lara, he always staunchly defended his marriage.

'You and Doctor Daniels must be very close,' Anna murmured.

'Yes. Yes, we have been.'

The reply was automatic but the truth was, Tony no longer knew where he stood with Lara.

She'd called him twice but he hadn't seen her — until last night. He'd been walking past the harbour when he'd seen her with Magnus, who must have got back from Buckie yesterday.

Lara had been sitting on the harbour wall, with Magnus standing behind her, a hand on her shoulder, pointing out to the *Ermingerd*, talking to her . . . Her face, looking up at him, had been so alive; Tony's heart had turned over.

Lara had always been there and he hadn't imagined a time when she wouldn't be. He realised how much he'd taken her for granted.

After the accident, Lara's face had been the first he'd seen. It had been Lara who told him about Jane, Lara who had cried with him, Lara who had forced him to pick up the pieces of his life.

Without her, he felt totally lost . . .

'Never worry about talking to Lara about anything,' he told Anna now. 'Anything at all that's bothering you.'

'I won't,' Anna promised.

'And if you need to talk — I'm not your doctor but if you need to talk to a friend, call me.'

Tony took a pen and an old raffle ticket from his pocket, and wrote his phone number on it. 'Call me,' he said.

★　★　★

164

Magnus sat on his mother's kitchen table and watched her take a cake out of the oven. 'Tired, old, almost ill,' Lara had said, and now that he was looking, Shona fitted the description. She seemed to be moving slower, more carefully.

'On Saturday, Lara's parents are coming to dinner,' she said.

'Yes, I know. Lara told me last night.'

'You'll be here?'

'I suppose so.' He smiled at her.

'I can't say I'm looking forward to it, either.' Shona leaned back against the sink. 'It seemed like a good idea, but the more I think about it . . . The only common ground Meg and I have any more is the Sutherlands and Anders. And I have the feeling it would be unwise to mention any of them.

'Still,' she added briskly, 'we have to make the effort for Lara's sake. Do you think it will go well? The visit, I mean?'

'I'd like to think so,' Magnus replied.

'I have my doubts, too,' Shona admitted. 'Lara thinks that Margaret just has to see Anders and we'll have the perfect fairytale ending.'

'I know, and it isn't going to be like that. I'm not just going on what Lara says, either. At Moira's funeral, remember? Margaret and Anders stood inches apart. At the time, I didn't take much notice, but they didn't exchange a single word.'

'Meg didn't say much to anyone,' Shona remembered. 'In fact, when Lara talks about her, I often think we're talking about two different people. The Meg Daniels I know . . . '

Shona's voice trailed away but Magnus knew exactly what she meant. The Meg Daniels they knew was cold, distant, and unfriendly.

'It's difficult to believe she's Anders' daughter,' Magnus said.

'Or Lara's mother!'

Shona began putting things away, and then glanced at the oven timer that she'd forgotten to set. She frowned.

'Mum, what's wrong?'

'Wrong? Why should there be anything wrong?'

'You look tired, and unwell. Lara noticed when she was here.'

'I don't know how,' Shona retorted, 'she was too busy getting your life story out of me. What's going on between you two, Magnus? I have Lara wanting to know everything about you. And then you tell me you saw her last night. What's going on?'

That was something else he'd noticed. His mother had been blessed with the patience of a saint but, lately, she'd been inclined to jump down people's throats for no reason at all.

'Nothing's going on! I called to see her last night, when I got back, and we went into Lerwick for a meal. Today we had lunch together. Later, when she's finished at the surgery, we're going down to Sumburgh. We're spending time together, that's all.'

'That's all?' his mother echoed dryly. Her searching gaze held his. 'You're in love with her, aren't you?'

Magnus nodded.

Shona gave a long, weary sigh. 'Oh, Magnus! Just look at the two of you. It would be impossible to find two people less suited. Do you honestly believe there's any future in it?'

Magnus choked back his temper. He could hear Lara's voice — 'She's your mum, she worries about you.'

'I think there could be, yes. I just wish she could get over this unnatural fear of the sea. But that's because she's grown up in the city. She's not used to it.'

'I've lived here all my life, Magnus, and I hate the sea. I always have and I always will.' He was shocked by that, she was pleased to see.

'It's different for you,' she went on. 'When you're out in a storm, it's an inconvenience.

167

For the women waiting at home . . . People tell me that you're one of the best, but sitting here, when there's a gale on, I get no comfort from your skill, the boat's safety, the radar, the radios — all I know is that you're in the hands of God. And all I can do is pray that He really has blessed all who sail in her.'

'Oh, Mum. You're too much of a worrier,' Magnus argued gently.

'I know, but when I think of Robbie . . . And it was different then. To your dad, it was a living. To you, the fishing's big business. He was never away as long as you, not so far away, either.'

'But look at the other crew wives. There are dozens of women who — '

'Of course there are,' Shona interrupted. 'It's a way of life, and the women here accept it. But Lara doesn't have to accept it.

'And what about Tony? I know things aren't going well between them, but they've been together a long time. Perhaps they'll kiss and make up. What then?'

Magnus was silent, and Shona's expression softened.

'I'm not saying anything against Lara, you know I'm not. I think the world of her. It's just that she comes from a different world, love. You'll be very different to anyone she's ever known. Now, if I thought she'd bring you

168

happiness, I'd be thrilled. But all I can see is heartbreak, Magnus.'

And all Magnus could see was Lara's face, smiling into his.

'What will you do, Magnus, if Lara marries Tony?' his mother's voice went on. 'How will you feel, living a stone's throw from them? How will you feel when you see them? How will you feel when you see their children? Will you be able to cope with that?'

Magnus looked up at last, and Shona's heart sank as she gazed into her son's eyes, which were full of pain.

'If it comes to that, then I'll have to, won't I, Mum? It's too late to say all this. Far too late. I can't change how I feel about her. Whatever happens, I love Lara — I'll love her for the rest of my life.'

7

Lara pushed open the door to Anders' house.

'It's only me,' she called out, 'and I've brought someone to see you.'

She had dreaded seeing disappointment on Anders' face, but she was in for a surprise. A light of recognition dawned in his eyes, and his face broke out in a warm smile.

'Robert!'

'No, don't get up,' Lara's father said, as Anders was about to stand. 'Margaret's just having her hair done, leaving me at a loose end. When Lara said she was coming to see you, I thought I'd join her — I hope you don't mind.'

The warmth and the mutual respect in their handshake brought a lump to Lara's throat.

'Your father is an exceptional man', Anders had said.

He certainly was! Lara could have hugged him for that kind lie — 'Margaret's just having her hair done . . . '. No one could have guessed that Margaret had refused to accompany them, or that she'd told them, in a voice bordering on hysteria, that she refused to be dragged around the island like a freak from a circus show. Come to that, Lara thought, no one would believe the way that Robert had put on his jacket and said to Margaret, very quietly but very firmly, 'I'm going to visit my father-in-law.'

Lara had thought that she was as close to her mother as a daughter could be. She'd imagined that she knew how Margaret would react in any situation. She couldn't have been more wrong. The woman she'd met at Sumburgh Airport was a stranger to her.

All the tension Margaret had shown, when Lara had told her she was moving to Shetland, had returned. She clearly hated being back.

The meal Shona had planned so carefully had been a disaster. Margaret had been stiffly polite and, on the rare occasions she'd spoken, she'd made it clear that she considered both Lara and Tony to be wasting their talents in Shetland. The way she spoke, it was only a matter of time before they both came to their senses and returned to London, where their skills could be put to good use.

It had been left to Robert, Magnus and Alisdair to make any real conversation. Fortunately, they'd had a long discussion on the difference that the Sullom Voe oil terminal had made to Shetland . . .

'Well, it's good to see you.' Robert was sitting beside Anders now.

'I'll put the kettle on,' Lara said softly.

'That's always her first job — put the kettle on.' She heard Anders' voice drift through from the sitting-room. 'What she really does is snoop round my cupboards and check that I've been taking all my pills and potions!'

'Anders! I heard that!' Lara called back. Her hand stilled on the cupboard door where he kept his medicines. And yes, because he wouldn't discuss his health with her, she always looked to see what he'd been prescribed. But how did he know?

She carried the tray into the sitting-room and moved a small table to put it on. The other table was covered in letters, papers, and maps.

'Here.' Anders handed her an old, faded photograph.

'This is it?' Lara asked, surprised. 'This is the shield? But it's so tiny.'

'The Kristiansund Jewel.' His eyes had a faraway look to them. 'And where is it now?'

At the bottom of the sea, Lara suspected.

'Are you sure that this is what your brother was bringing to Shetland?' she asked.

'Not absolutely. But Jakob was nervous and worried when I last spoke to him. We only spoke for about five minutes. I asked him

172

what he was doing but, of course, he wouldn't tell me. It was safer not to know.

'But he did say that, if he didn't get back, Kristiansund would never forgive him . . . then he added that the whole of Norway would never forgive him. That was enough to tell me.

'Then he seemed to push it all from his mind,' Anders went on, remembering those brief minutes with his brother. 'He wanted to know how we'd managed to hide the ammunition we'd just delivered. He had me showing him the hold where it had been hidden.'

'Perhaps he was trying to find a hiding place on his own boat,' Robert suggested.

'Perhaps,' Anders agreed. 'But I had the feeling he didn't trust the skipper. People feared for their safety, for their families . . . It was difficult to trust anyone.' He looked at them both. 'Jakob never put the shield on that boat. I *know* he didn't.'

'It's such a long time ago,' Robert said, his gaze still on the photograph.

Anders nodded. 'And I'd forgotten all about it. As soon as I heard that Jakob was dead, everything else went out of my mind — we'd always been so close, you see. I suppose I deliberately remembered only the good times.'

Lara took his hand.

'But the night I saw the film, the night I saw you, Lara, it all came back to me,' Anders went on. 'I was thinking of Moira mostly, but my thoughts were also with those who'd given their lives. That's when I remembered those final minutes with Jakob.'

'The boat he was on,' Robert mused. 'Was it ever salvaged?'

'No. It was just a small, worthless fishing boat.

'A friend in Norway, Hugo, is trying to find out what other boats left at the same time. Also, I'm in touch with the museums. Most believe that the shield was lost with Jakob, or that it fell into enemy hands. But I don't.'

Her grandfather was worn out. Lara wished he would forget all about this shield. Magnus was right — it was becoming an obsession with him.

'I want to know the truth,' Anders explained, as if he could read her thoughts. 'Not for myself so much as for Jakob. He never had the chance to experience life, or to leave something of himself behind . . . he never knew the joy of children.' His eyes rested on Lara. 'Or grandchildren.

'If I could just discover that the shield was safely tucked away, then I would know that

Jakob's life hadn't been entirely in vain.'

'Yes,' Robert said softly, 'I can understand that.'

'Your tea's getting cold,' Lara said, practically, and Anders smiled.

'She keeps you in order, too, then?' Robert joked.

Anders and her father got along well. What a terrible waste, Lara thought again. If only things had been different, Anders could have given so much to their family . . . But then there was Margaret.

Robert, like herself, was keeping an eye on Anders' energy levels. It wasn't long before he rose to go.

'I hope you'll be able to come again before you leave the islands,' Anders told him.

'I'll look forward to it. Margaret will come, too.' Only Lara noticed the hard edge to his voice.

'Thank you,' Anders said gruffly, 'for coming today and for — ' His voice dropped to a whisper. 'For Lara, too.'

Smiling, Robert clasped his hand.

'I don't think Margaret and I can take all the credit. There's a lot of her grandfather in her!'

★ ★ ★

Magnus and Lara walked through the town to the harbour. The *Ermingerd* was alongside, patiently waiting for morning.

Magnus stopped in front of the boat, gazing at it with a look of what could only be described as affection.

'Beautiful, isn't she?'

Lara tried to look at the boat dispassionately. Instead of a vessel responsible for the lives of Magnus, Alisdair and the rest of the crew, she tried to see it as a feat of engineering. And still she could see no beauty. It seemed top heavy, as if the first wave would knock it straight onto its side.

It was getting late as they carried on walking.

'What or where is Ermingerd?' Lara asked curiously, and Magnus smiled.

'She was the queen of Narbonne, in France, back in the twelfth century. Earl Rognvald met her on his way to — you know about Earl Rognvald?'

Lara shook her head.

'He was one of the Norse earls, who had the cathedral built in Orkney. Saint Magnus was his uncle.

'Anyway, Rognvald met Ermingerd on his way to the Holy Land. The people wanted him to marry her but he decided to continue on his journey, promising to call at

Narbonne on the way back.

'He wrote a lot of poetry about her. Anyway he returned to Norway and then there was trouble in Orkney that had to be dealt with. He never went back to France.

'I believe, though,' he added softly, 'that she was forever in his heart.

'Rognvald was one of the few earls who visited Shetland. He wrecked two of his longships at Gulberwick. I'll take you sometime and show you the exact spot.'

'You certainly know how to show a girl a good time!' Lara teased.

Magnus laughed too but any reply he was going to make was forgotten as they turned the corner and practically collided with Tony. Anna Thompson was with him.

Lara was speechless. Her heart began to pound with temper, but she couldn't utter a word.

'Hello,' Tony said quietly, and Magnus spoke, first to Anna, then to Tony.

Lara's patient looked at her. Her eyes wouldn't quite meet Lara's, and her usually pale face flushed with embarrassment. Her hand had been resting lightly on Tony's arm, but she quickly moved it to her side.

How could Tony do it? He knew! He was the one who'd sent Anna for medical help. Tony knew that the last thing Anna needed at the moment was emotional involvement.

Not only that, he'd even had the cheek to tell Lara that she'd been wrong in referring Anna for counselling . . .

'I need to talk to you, Tony.' Lara's voice shook with anger. 'Tomorrow. I'll be at the surgery at eight-thirty. Will you ring me then, before surgery starts?'

'Yes, of course.'

'Thank you. Goodnight, then. Goodnight, Anna.'

As they walked back to Magnus's car, Lara began to calm down. Magnus, glancing at her, held his peace.

Lara knew she'd acted in a totally unprofessional way. Perhaps she shouldn't have been so hard on Tony. He was, she knew, quite unaware that girls fell for him as easily as they took their next breath . . .

As Magnus drove her home, however, she put herself in Anna's shoes. What would it do to Anna, spending the evening with such an attractive man?

She was jolted out of her thoughts when Magnus stopped the car outside Bay View.

'Are you coming in?'

'No. I honestly don't think I could cope with a dose of your mother.'

The bitter edge to his voice surprised Lara. He got out of the car and came round to open her door, as if he couldn't get rid of her quickly enough.

They hadn't spoken, she realised. She'd been too wrapped up in her thoughts to notice but, since seeing Tony and Anna, they hadn't exchanged a single word.

'What's wrong, Magnus?'

'With me? Nothing. But I haven't just seen the love of my life with someone else, have I?'

Was that how it had seemed? But her concern had been for Anna — her patient. Until this moment, the fact that Tony had been with someone else hadn't even registered.

It should have, she'd spent years longing for him to love her . . . but seeing Tony with someone else had meant nothing to her.

'It wasn't like that, Magnus,' she said quietly.

'No?'

Lara shook her head.

'So how was it?' Magnus demanded.

Lara gazed back at him helplessly. How could she break confidentiality?

'I don't like playing games, Lara.'

His anger didn't quite manage to conceal the hurt in his eyes. Lara put a hand on his arm but he brushed it aside.

'If you want to use someone to get back at

Tony.' he said harshly, 'you can choose someone else.'

'That's not fair!' Lara cried.

'Isn't it?'

'No. I'm not using anyone, or playing games. I've been completely honest with you, Magnus. I told you from the start that I wouldn't get involved with you.'

'Yes,' he said at last, 'I suppose you did.'

'There's no suppose about it. If you want to see me, fine. If you don't want to see me, that's fine too. But don't accuse me of using you!'

He gazed back at her for a long time. Then, without saying a word, he turned away. With the driver's door open, he paused.

'I might see you when I get back, and I might not. As you say, it doesn't much matter either way, does it?'

He got in the car and drove off.

'But it does matter,' Lara whispered to the still night air.

She stood where he'd left her, waiting to see his car coming back along the road. She couldn't believe he could leave like that. Not when they'd spent a perfect evening together, not when he was leaving in the morning. Not when it would be days before they saw each other again . . .

Next day, Margaret Daniels sat uneasily in Lara's car outside Braeside, her old home. The place housed memories she had spent most of her life trying to forget. There, on the drive, was Magnus Cameron's car.

'I thought you said Magnus was away,' she said sharply.

'He is,' Lara answered. 'He takes the Land Rover. Shona uses the car when he's at the fishing.'

Margaret breathed a sigh of relief. It was bad enough that Lara had bullied her into coming — 'There's something I want you to see', she'd said — but she couldn't have tolerated seeing Magnus Cameron as well.

She didn't have anything against him personally, but he was a Shetlander. She didn't like the way he looked at Lara, either, and even worse was the way Lara looked at him.

She hadn't forgotten the dinner at Shona's, when Lara had gone into the kitchen to make coffee, and Magnus had made an excuse to follow her.

Margaret had thought nothing of it until she heard Lara's sudden shriek of laughter. 'Magnus, put me down!' she'd cried. And that had been followed by a silence that had been even more unnerving.

Robert had looked mildly surprised. Shona's lips had compressed into a tight line of disapproval. Alisdair's grin had started at one ear and gone right round to the other.

Margaret had been shocked beyond words. She'd been convinced Lara would, in the end, settle down with Tony. Lara wasn't the type to indulge in childish infatuation, and yet, unless Margaret was mistaken, that was exactly what she was doing. She couldn't even begin to understand it. What was there about Magnus that might appeal to her daughter? When it came to the bottom line, he was a fisherman. A fisherman!

It wasn't that she wanted something better for Lara, exactly. She just wanted someone compatible. Like Tony.

'Let's go inside,' Lara suggested.

Taking a deep breath, Margaret got out of the car. She would endure this for Lara's sake.

The first thing that struck her about Braeside was how different the house was. It was lighter, brighter and less cluttered. Nevertheless, memories still lingered around every corner.

'Lara, I don't think — after all, it's someone else's home now . . . .'

'Rubbish,' Lara scoffed. 'Magnus doesn't

mind. When he gave me the keys, he said we could come any time.'

'Even so, it's not right.'

Lara urged her mother towards the conservatory.

'Through here. Sit and look through these old photos with me.'

Back in London, Lara and her mother would have delighted in poring over old photographs. But not here. Once again, Lara was sitting with a stranger.

Margaret chose to remember very little about the photos of her childhood or when they were taken. Putting them aside, Lara found the letters Iain Sutherland had written to his wife, Moira, during the war.

'We found these,' she said quietly.

'We? Who's we?'

'Magnus found them,' Lara said reluctantly.

'Magnus Cameron?' Margaret exploded. 'What does any of this have to do with him?'

Lara threw the letters onto the table and rounded on her mother.

'It has everything to do with him. All this — ' her wild gesture took in the letters, photographs, paintings, ornaments — 'all this is yours. Magnus doesn't want it. Nothing would make him happier than to come home and find it had all gone.

'Much as he loved your mother, all this stuff is cluttering up his home. You should have dealt with it. You!'

She took a deep breath, trying to calm herself

'You can't blame the entire population of Shetland for what happened when you were a child, Mum. You can't blame Magnus, you can't blame Alisdair, you can't blame Shona, you can't blame Fiona in the shop . . . '

Margaret's colour was high, and so it should be, Lara thought.

'If you insist on having someone to blame,' she added more quietly, 'then you should blame your mother. If she'd married Anders, as he begged her to, everything would have been different. She believed that what she was doing was right for Iain, and perhaps it was, but it wasn't right for the rest of us.'

Lara's eyes strayed to the window, to the stunning view out over the voe and she sighed.

'I think she felt duty bound to stay with Iain. And I think that, so long as she had Anders' love, she could suffer anything.' She was speaking almost to herself, until a small sound from her mother made her look round.

'Oh, Mum,' Lara whispered, 'why are we arguing? You and me? We never argue. We've always been such — such good friends.'

Margaret reached out for Lara's hand and squeezed it tightly in her own.

'We're not arguing, darling. It's just that we see two different people. You look at Anders Larsen and you see an old, sick man.'

'No. I see a man who considers himself lucky to have such a wide circle of friends — when we both know that having friends owes nothing to luck. I see a loving, gentle man with a warm sense of humour. I see a man who loves me unconditionally, who loves me because I'm part of him and a part of Moira. I see a man who almost welcomes death because he firmly believes that then, he will finally be with the woman he's loved all his life . . .'

Margaret stood up and walked over to the long low window. Her stiff back was to Lara.

'What do you see, Mum?'

She thought her mother wasn't going to reply, but she did.

'I see a reckless, thoughtless, selfish man. A man who came, changed my mother into the happiest person alive, and then went away again. He went away!' Margaret's voice broke. 'I spent years craving love from that man. I never got it.'

'But you did!' Lara said urgently. 'You've always had it. If you had nothing else, you had Anders' love. You still have it.'

Margaret turned around and shook her head. There were tears in her eyes.

Lara wanted to go to her mother. The house was feeling oppressive. She could sense Moira's presence. Lara wished that Magnus would walk through the door and bring the place back to life. But she knew he wouldn't.

'I suppose my mother did the best she could, Lara, but that wasn't much. She loved me but she never had time for me. Iain saw to that. He made demands on her, he resented anything or anyone that kept her away from his beck and call. She couldn't let me make a mess, make a noise — 'my dad' didn't like it.

'I remember so well the day Anders told Iain — the shock of learning that I wasn't Iain's daughter at all . . .

'When the shock wore off, everything fell into place. Suddenly, everything made sense. Iain didn't love me because I wasn't his daughter. He shouted and screamed at me because I wasn't his daughter.'

The tears were pouring down Margaret's face now, but Lara felt sure her mother was unaware of them.

'I decided that if I was Anders' daughter, he must love me. To my naive twelve-year-old mind, that was logical. After all, fathers loved their daughters, didn't they? I was happy. Finally, I had a father to love me.'

Lara wished she could close her ears. Goosebumps had broken out on her skin and she knew that if she closed her eyes for a second, she would hear Moira's voice, or Iain, screaming at Margaret . . .

And still Margaret's hoarse voice went on. Still the tears poured down her face . . .

'I'd been given new ribbons. I spent ages that morning, tying them in my hair. I wanted Anders to see what a pretty daughter he had. Red ribbons, they were, red with tiny white stars on them.

'I left here and walked all the way to his house. I suppose that was the happiest walk I ever took. It's what? — five? six miles? And all the way, I marvelled at the experience that awaited me. I was so happy at the thought of finally having a father who would show me a little love — just a little. God knows, I wasn't greedy.

'I stood at his door — I don't know how long I stood there. Finally, Mrs Ashby came out of her house — she lived next door — and told me that he'd gone back to Norway.

'I didn't believe her at first. He'd only arrived the day before. But it was true. He'd dropped his bombshell and was on his way back, leaving us to pick up the pieces.'

Margaret brushed her tears away, but fresh

ones quickly followed.

'So I walked back home.' Her voice struggled with overwhelming emotion. 'I took the cliff path back. I tore those stupid ribbons from my hair and threw them over the cliff.

'I remember I stood and watched the wind take them right to the bottom. And I wished I'd been brave enough to follow them down.'

Lara rushed forward and hugged her mother close. At last Margaret began to sob, and as Lara held her, the past slowly left them, and the sun slid from behind a dark cloud, filling Moira's house with sunshine once more . . .

* * *

Lara had made every excuse imaginable that week to drive past the harbour and finally, she saw what she was looking for. The *Ermingerd* was back in port.

The relief was immense, and she knew a sudden rush of affection for the top-heavy lump of metal.

Without pausing to think, she drove straight to Braeside. Yes, there was the Land Rover, parked next to his car.

Lara got out of her car and went and hammered on his door. Getting no response, she tried the door. It was unlocked, so she went inside and called his name.

Silence.

She wandered into the conservatory and gazed out towards the water, but there was no sign of him.

She was in the hall, on her way out, when the door swept open and there stood Magnus.

Lara felt suddenly ridiculous, like Goldilocks caught trespassing.

'I was looking for you — the door was open,' she blurted out.

He nodded. 'I saw the car,' he said coldly.

Lara had imagined this would be so easy. She'd thought he would be as pleased to see her as she was to see him. She'd imagined that there would be little need for explanations.

Instead, she found herself faced with that expression she detested. Except it wasn't even an expression. It was like a mask drawn by a small child who'd forgotten that mouths curled up if they were happy or down if they were sad.

'Magnus, about what happened — '

She looked at him in mute appeal but he just stared back at her. Nothing was different, she realised. She *still* couldn't give him a sensible explanation. Fool that she was, she hadn't realised that she would have to.

'I realise how it must have seemed,' she

blundered on, 'but it wasn't like that at all. I can't explain, I'm afraid, but the fact that Tony was with someone else wasn't what annoyed me. It was something quite different.'

He was still impassive. It was as if he had an internal switch on his feelings, and was capable of switching it on or off at will.

'I *wasn't* using you, Magnus. I wasn't playing games. I was with you because I wanted to be with you. I'm here now for the same reason.'

At last she got a reaction — a typical Magnus reaction. One moment she didn't have the faintest idea what he was thinking, and the next she could see right through his soul.

'I hope so, Lara, because I'll tell you this now.' He strode forward and his hands clamped themselves onto her arms. 'If ever you walk up the aisle to Tony Adams, you'll be stepping over my dead body to get to him!'

His harsh words shook Lara to the core, but then she felt his warm breath on her face as he whispered her name. Gentle hands cupped her face. His kiss was so exquisitely tender that it brought tears of wonder to her eyes.

He must have understood, because he held her close, stroking her hair, and occasionally kissing the top of her head. The silly quarrel, the emptiness of the last few days, dissolved into nothing. There was only Magnus.

'You're Anna's doctor, aren't you?' he said suddenly.

The spell was broken.

Lara's arms dropped to her sides. Realising with some surprise that they were still standing in the hall, she took a step back into the kitchen.

'You know I can't discuss — '

'I know,' he said.

She was surprised and relieved that he didn't push the issue, but then she realised that he had no need to. He'd come up with the explanation he wanted, and he was satisfied.

'What was Anna like, Magnus, before her grandfather died?'

'I'll take that as professional interest and not plain nosiness.' he replied dryly.

He rubbed a thoughtful finger across his chin. *I love the way he does that*, Lara thought.

'She was much the same as she is now,' Magnus said. 'But less fragile. She was always painfully shy, naive, and too trusting for her own good. Her mother left home when she was very young and then her father died. Her grandfather was a marvellous old chap but I don't suppose it was an ideal situation for Anna.

'She started seeing someone who worked at Sullom Voe,' he went on. 'Jonathan Armstrong. He was — ' He pulled a face. 'He was a pretty loathsome — actually, now I come to think about it, he was a lot like Tony.'

'Magnus!' Lara exclaimed with exasperation. 'You can't possibly dislike Tony. There's nothing in Tony to dislike!'

Magnus was taken aback.

'No, I don't dislike him but — ' He shrugged. 'I suppose I'm jealous. I look at him and see everything you should want. And I look at him and see everything I'm not.'

His frankness surprised Lara, and touched her, too.

'But I actually meant that they're alike in looks. Both tall, both with that fair hair, both smart.'

'They planned to marry, didn't they? This Jonathan Armstrong and Anna?'

'Anna might have planned marriage,' Magnus said grimly, 'but Armstrong certainly didn't. He went off to Canada, leaving a string of abandoned women behind him. Life was one big ego trip for him. He cared for no one but himself.'

'Poor Anna,' Lara murmured.

'I imagine it was the humiliation that hit

192

her harder than anything else. She locked herself away from everyone, and then her grandfather was ill — it was the perfect excuse for keeping the world at arm's length. She never had to go out and face everyone. And now . . . '

And now she wasn't able to.

Lara sincerely hoped that Tony knew what he was getting into — for his sake and for Anna's. He'd said he felt sorry for Anna which was why he'd asked her out. He'd also told Lara that he'd been feeling a little lost . . .

Her pager bleeped, and she groaned.

'I'm on call,' she said apologetically, lifting the phone.

She smiled as she listened, guessing that Connie, an over-anxious mother-to-be, was suffering from yet another attack of indigestion. They would all breathe a sigh of relief when this baby was born.

'I'll be there.' She replaced the receiver. 'I've got to go, Magnus. I'll call you later . . . '

It was more than four hours later, just after ten, when Lara finally got home that evening. Connie's indigestion had passed but it had taken Lara a while to reassure her that all was well. Then she'd been called to two more patients.

Her parents were still out. Robert had

finally persuaded Margaret to 'go for a drive' and Lara hoped, although she wasn't too optimistic, that it was proving enjoyable.

There were two messages on her answerphone and she hit the button as she took off her jacket.

The first voice was plaintive.

'Who can possibly need you more than I do?' Magnus wanted to know, and she laughed happily.

'I'm going to see Anders,' he went on, 'so if you ring and I'm not here, I'll be there.' She heard the amusement in his voice as he added, 'Or I'll be somewhere in between.'

The second voice immediately took the smile from her face.

'Lara . . . Lara, I don't know what to do . . .'

It was Fran — her cousin, her best friend, and yet, because of the terrible sobbing, Lara struggled to recognise the voice. There was a huge, gulping breath.

'Lara, please call me . . . Quickly . . .'

And the tape ran on, bringing to Lara the frightening sound of Fran's weeping.

8

Lara's call was answered almost immediately.

'Fran? It's me. What's happened?'

'Lara!' Fran had sounded calm as she'd recited her number, but now the sobbing started all over again. 'My flat — '

'Calm down,' Lara said gently, 'and tell me what's happened.'

'I went out this morning,' Fran said, her voice shaking, 'and when I came back at lunchtime . . . ' She took a huge gulp of air. 'Someone had broken in. In broad daylight. The mess — everything was a mess.'

'No! What was taken?'

'Television, video recorder, clock, camera . . . And you know the bracelet Gran gave me on my twenty-first?'

'Oh no!' Lara groaned.

'Yes. The black cat that Phil gave me when I took my driving test — they smashed that. Oh, Lara, I wish you were here.'

So did Lara.

'What about Uncle John and Aunt Sophie?' she asked gently. 'Have they been round?'

'Yes, they came straight over. I'd already called the police by then, so I had a houseful.

195

But now they've gone. You know how easy it is to be brave when there are people about, but as soon as they'd gone ... I know it's only a few possessions but — '

'I know,' Lara agreed sympathetically. 'Gran's bracelet and Phil's cat weren't just possessions though, were they? What did the police say?'

'Nothing,' Fran replied with a sigh, 'except that there had been several break-ins in the area, and that I'd be lucky to see any of it again.' The sobbing started again. 'I've been sitting by the phone too scared to do anything. Every time I hear a noise — '

'Why not spend the night with your mum and dad?' Lara suggested.

'They're upset enough as it is, and I don't want them fussing. I wish you were here. Lara.'

Lara wished she was, too. Fran, she knew, was hopeless in a crisis. And Lara suspected that if her home had been broken into, and her treasured possessions stolen or broken, she'd be no better.

Well, if she couldn't go to Fran ...

'Ring the airport,' she said briskly, 'and see if you can get on the morning plane. I expect you can. Just pack a suitcase — '

'I can't,' Fran wailed. 'My clothes were all over the floor, all pulled out of the wardrobe and out of the drawers. Some were even torn. My clothes, Lara. Even my clothes!'

'You've still got the keys to my flat,' Lara pointed out. 'Spend the night there. Mum said it's just how I left it, so there will be a few clothes there, and they'll fit you — we've been the same size since we were fourteen. Take what you want. Just get on that plane. OK?'

'But you've got Auntie Margaret and Uncle Rob there,' Fran said. 'You don't want me as well.'

Lara smiled at the half-hearted refusal. 'Of course I do. In fact, I could do with someone to talk to . . .'

★ ★ ★

Two days later, Lara decided that Fran's visit was the best thing that could have happened. Shetland seemed to have worked its own special magic.

'I felt better as soon as I got on the plane,' her cousin admitted sheepishly. 'You shouldn't run away from things, I know, but away up here, I can get it into perspective and then go back and face it.'

Lara saw that her mother was more relaxed with Fran about the place, too. Perhaps Fran's presence made Margaret feel closer to home, or perhaps fussing over her took her mind off everything else.

Lara grinned to herself as she stopped her car outside Shona's house and picked up an envelope from the passenger seat.

Shona had called at Little Bay that morning. Lara had missed her but Margaret had passed on the message about the raffle tickets she needed back.

Lara walked into the kitchen and found Shona giving Rachel Thompson, Anna's five-year-old daughter, a lesson in the art of pastry making.

'Mummy's at the hospital so I'm helping Shona,' Rachel explained importantly.

'Lucky Shona,' Lara replied with a smile. 'You'll have to come and help me one day, Rachel. I can't make pastry.'

'Can't you?' Rachel's eyes were wide.

'No.'

Shaking her head in astonishment, blonde curls bobbing, Rachel concentrated on rolling out her pastry.

'I'm glad you came to the rescue, Shona. Anna had been wondering who'd look after Rachel when she went to the hospital for these appointments.'

'Yes. As soon as I heard, I practically begged her.' Shona's fond eyes rested on Rachel. 'I'm only too glad to help out. I miss having children about the place, and I've resigned myself to never having grand-children.'

'You can't discount that idea yet,' Lara murmured.

'Well, I have.'

'Raffle tickets.' Lara put the envelope on the dresser.

'It didn't warrant a special journey, love. Did you manage to sell many?'

'All of them.' She laughed at Shona's surprise. 'All thanks to Liz. We put them on the reception desk at the surgery and I think it was a case of buy a raffle ticket or wait a mighty long time to see a doctor.'

'Good old Liz.' Shona laughed.

A car stopped outside, and she peered out of the kitchen window.

'There are three of them,' she told Rachel with amusement. 'We'll have no food left.'

Magnus and Ivan, his crewman, walked into the kitchen.

Lara was working, she'd only called in as she was passing, and seeing Magnus was an unexpected joy. He looked at her, with that certain look he had, and then, like Ivan, turned his attention to Rachel.

'Hello, stranger,' he said, ruffling her curls. 'Is all this food for me?'

'No,' Rachel replied firmly, 'it has to be shared.'

Magnus helped himself to an apple turnover. 'Did you make this?'

'Yes.'

Rachel watched eagerly as he ate it.

'You'll have to marry me,' Magnus declared, wiping his mouth.

'You know I can't,' Rachel chided. 'I've already promised Ally that I'll marry him.'

Magnus laughed. 'So you have.'

'It's OK. I've found — Hey!' Alisdair swept into the room, lifted Rachel off her feet and swung her in the air. 'Princess! What are you doing here?'

Her flour-covered hands gripped his shoulders as she laughed happily.

'I'm helping Shona. Mummy's taking me home at five o'clock.'

'I might not let her,' Alisdair said gravely. 'I might keep you here all to myself.'

'You'd have to take me on your boat with you.'

'So I would,' Alisdair agreed.

'Would you let me steer?' The child's face was a picture of happiness.

'Of course.'

'And if I got bored with that, could I catch a fish?'

'Only one?' Alisdair laughed.

'You can take my place any time,' Ivan told her, and Rachel looked at him.

'Do you get seasick?'

'All the time,' Ivan assured her.

When Alisdair reluctantly put the child down, there was a look in his eyes that completely took Lara by surprise. It was almost wistful. He caught her watching him and that wistful expression was quickly replaced by the carefree grin that they all knew so well. Strangely though, it didn't seem quite as carefree as it usually did.

Lara would have liked to stay for the rest of the day but she had work to do. When Magnus and Ivan were leaving, there was no longer any reason to stay. She walked to the cars with them.

'Are you really seasick, Ivan?' she asked curiously.

'Sick of the sea,' he retorted. 'I hate it!'

'You hate the sea? You don't like fishing?' Lara was amazed.

'Like fishing?' Ivan smiled. 'Only a madman would like fishing!'

'Oh, but I thought — '

Ivan turned to face her.

'You're away from home for days on end. You've got force nines, swells of thirty feet or more, seas that would kill a man in minutes ... it has to be the most miserable job in the world.'

Magnus looked at Lara's pale face, and scowled at his crewmate.

'It's not always like that.'

'No? So why does nobody dare whistle on deck? Why does nobody wave us off? Why do we all live in fear of seeing the minister strolling alongside? And why does every last one of us take a blasted pebble with us?'

Magnus shrugged.

'Superstition dies hard, but I still say it's not that bad.'

'Not for the skipper,' Ivan countered, 'all warm, dry and cosy in the wheelhouse.'

'Then get your skipper's ticket,' Magnus retorted.

'Aye. And how much would that cost me? Besides, what's the point? The fishing industry's as good as dead.'

'Rubbish!' Magnus scoffed. 'We've always fished, and we always will. It'll take more than a few EC directives to stop that!'

'Take no notice.' Ivan grinned at Lara. 'We have this argument at least once a week.'

'Are you working?' Magnus asked Lara, changing the subject.

'I've got one more patient to see. I was going to call on you when I'd finished.'

'I'm just dropping Ivan off, then I'll be home. I'll get the coffee ready . . . '

It was an hour later when Lara finished for the day and, true to his word, Magnus had coffee ready and waiting. He looked edgy, Lara thought.

They carried their coffee into the conservatory and sat facing the water, enjoying the view that Moira had loved so much.

'I think Rachel's in love with your brother,' Lara remarked with a chuckle.

'I think the feeling's mutual.' Magnus gave his slow smile.

'Did you see the way he looked? He looked — well, wistful.'

'Wistful?' The idea seemed to amuse Alisdair's big brother. 'Perhaps he's feeling his age. Perhaps he thinks it's high time he settled down and had children of his own.' He frowned suddenly. 'Now I come to think of it, I think Anna's name's in his wee black book. They had a bit of thing going at one time?'

'When?'

'Years back. And it has to be said that Ally's had a bit of a thing with a lot of girls. It's probably ten years ago now.'

'What happened?' Lara asked curiously and Magnus was thoughtful.

'I don't know, but it didn't last long. And I

don't suppose it meant anything to either of them.'

'Oh.' Lara would have dismissed the whole thing if it hadn't been for that unguarded expression on Alisdair's face . . .

'Does Ivan really hate fishing?' she asked, breaking the thoughtful silence.

Magnus stood up and walked to the window, blocking out some of the light.

'I think he can take it or leave it. He was working south once and caught his hand in a winch. His arm was broken in a couple of places. They tried to get a helicopter out, but the conditions were too bad. It was about sixteen hours before the boat reached land. I think that put him off.'

Lara shuddered. 'I'm not surprised.'

He swung round. 'But it's not nearly as bad as he made out.'

Seas that would kill a man in minutes.

'I know what it's like, Magnus.'

But she didn't. Not really.

'I know the women never wave their menfolk off,' she said, 'but what's all this about pebbles?'

'You take a pebble from the beach,' he explained with obvious reluctance, 'the best you can find, and the trows, the good spirits, bring you safely home so that you can return it.'

'Do *you* take a pebble?' she asked, unable to imagine anyone less superstitious than Magnus.

He nodded.

'And why can't you whistle?'

'Because you might whistle up the wind.'

'And the minister?' she asked in amazement.

'If the minister is the last person to see you leave, he'll be the first person to see you return — and you might be in a box.' He shrugged. 'It's all superstitious nonsense.'

'But you still take a pebble?'

'I was taking a pebble before you were born,' he told her, 'when Dad still had to lift me onto the boat. By the time I was old enough to realise it was ridiculous, it had become a habit.'

'Heavens!' Her voice was brimming with amusement. 'This fishing business is a lot more complex than I realised.'

Magnus returned the smile, but Lara had the feeling that it had taken a great deal of effort.

He gazed out across the water once more. Lara went and stood by his side, wondering why he was so unsettled. His arm went round her shoulders and he seemed to relax a little.

'Why does Ivan do it if he dislikes it so much?' she asked.

'Because it's what he's always done. A lot of men say they hate it, but they still do it. Besides,' he added with a smile, 'he has a wife and half a child to support.'

She laughed softly.

Yesterday, she'd examined Marie and, together, they'd listened to that 'half a child's' heartbeat. Marie had frowned with concentration as Lara handed her the stethoscope and then her face had been alight with wonder. Tears had shone in her eyes.

Lara had known a brief but very intense pang of envy. She'd always wanted children, but she had never before felt envious. Perhaps, having reached the grand age of thirty, her biological clock was reminding her that the years were passing. Whatever the reason, wanting children was changing to a longing for them.

She leaned her head against Magnus's shoulder as she thought how things had come full circle. She and Magnus had met as children in this very house, walked along that beach down there.

Today the beach was deserted but, one day, other children would be there. Marie's child . . .

She felt it again, that sharp stab of envy. Yesterday, she would have given all she had to be in Marie's place, to know that a child was growing inside her.

Not *a* child, an inner voice whispered. Her child — and Magnus's. *Their* child.

She turned her shocked face to his and what she saw in his eyes shocked her even more. She knew, as clearly as if the words were branded across his face, that he was thinking exactly the same thing . . .

'I'm going out to dinner with Tony tonight,' she blurted out.

His arm dropped from her shoulder. 'Yes. I know.'

'You know?' Lara was astonished. 'How?'

'Mum saw your mother this morning and I gather Margaret was shouting it from the rooftops. Anyway, Mum decided it warranted a phone call.'

Lara understood now. She wondered what bothered him most; the fact that she was going, the fact that Margaret had shouted it from the rooftops, or the fact that Shona had decided it warranted a phone call.

'Yes, well — all mothers want to see their children married off. Mum's hoping I'll come to my senses and marry Tony.'

'And will you?'

'Come to my senses,' Lara joked, 'or marry Tony?'

There was no smile from Magnus.

'Marry Tony.'

207

'No.'

'Why?'

'For one thing, he hasn't asked me, and for another, I don't love him. If I loved him, I wouldn't be here, would I?'

'I don't know, Lara.' He gazed at her for a long time. 'You know what they say about absence making the heart grow fonder and all that.'

'Like it has with Fran and Alisdair? I expected — well, I don't know what I expected but when Fran was here before, they spent every minute together. Now there's nothing.'

'According to Ally, they had a lot of fun but they don't have anything in common. Although why everyone is so obsessed with having things in common,' he added darkly, 'I can't imagine. Look at Anders and Moira. Everyone knows they should have married and what did they have in common? Nothing! When they met they couldn't even speak the same language.'

'That's true,' Lara murmured. 'I've been trying to find something we had in common and I thought there was nothing . . . at least we speak the same language, I suppose.'

'Aye,' he agreed with a sudden laugh. 'An du minds me aafil o dee graandfaider, hinny.'

She laughed happily, slipped her arms

around his waist and lifted her face for his kiss. She heard his soft sigh as his lips touched hers, a sigh that said 'we can't go on like this'. And her heart sighed too, because she knew he was right . . .

★ ★ ★

The food that evening was delicious, conversation flowed easily, laughter abounded, and Lara was a million miles away. Or if not a million, certainly a few.

She hadn't told Magnus that her parents and Fran were also having dinner with them. He was sure to know. Their mothers' grapevine would have seen to that.

It didn't matter, she told herself. Whether he knew or not wasn't important. And yet her mind refused to budge from the fact that she hadn't told him.

She dragged her mind back to the table. Tony and Fran were sharing a joke, and Robert was laughing with them. Margaret was watching Lara with an expression of something approaching despair . . .

It was late when they reached Lara's home, but not that late.

'I think I'll turn in,' Margaret said briskly.

'Hmm? Oh yes, me too,' Robert agreed immediately.

'Yes, I want an early night, too.' Fran quickly grabbed a paperback, and headed for her room.

Less than a minute later, Lara and Tony were alone.

'You have a very tactful family,' Tony said, and then his smile faded.

'Lara, I've missed you,' he said softly. 'Nothing feels right anymore.'

Lara's heart sank. She couldn't tell him she'd missed him too. She *had* missed him but in a different way.

'I'm still here,' she said lightly.

'Is it about Anna?' he asked quietly.

'No, of course not.'

'It was stupid of me,' he admitted. 'I felt sorry for her, I suppose. I still do. And I felt lonely. But you're right, taking her out was a stupid thing to do.'

'It's not what she needs right now.' She smiled at him fondly. 'You have to remember, Tony, that women fall in love with you — ' she clicked her fingers, 'just like that.'

'You didn't.'

'But I did, Tony. I did.'

He lifted her chin with his finger, forcing her to look into those beautiful warm brown eyes.

'I love *you*, Lara. You know that.'

'No. You might love the idea of me and you

might love me as a friend, but it was Jane you loved. I could never have been more than the consolation prize.'

'Don't say that,' he groaned.

She had to say it, and they both knew it was true.

'I do love you, Tony, as a friend, as the dearest friend I'm ever likely to have. We've been through a lot — we've laughed together, cried together — of course I love you.

'Not so long ago, I spent half my time willing you to ask me to marry you. I couldn't push you, I knew it had to come from you. But now, I'm glad you didn't ask. We'd have lived to regret it.'

'Is it Magnus?' he asked gruffly.

Lara shook her head.

'You've been spending a lot of time with him, Lara.'

'Yes, but Magnus has nothing to do with how I feel about you, Tony. He's not the reason my feelings for you changed.'

'Is it serious?' he persisted. 'You and Magnus?'

Lara was unable to answer him.

'I see,' Tony murmured.

'No, you don't,' Lara answered softly. 'Tony, let's not spoil things. We've all had a lovely evening, we've always been good friends, and we always will be. We've never been more than friends though, not really. And now, we might not be seeing each other so often but nothing's changed.'

'Everything's changed, Lara.' His eyes were filled with sadness.

'No,' Lara argued. 'We were wrong to see so much of each other. One day, you'll meet someone else. Someone who makes you feel the way Jane made you feel.

'And who knows? I might meet Mr Right, and then again I might end up with a house full of cats.

'It's late, Tony,' she said quietly. 'I'll call you in a few days. OK?'

He gazed back at her for long moments. Finally, he nodded. She put her hand into his as they walked out to his car.

He was about to speak, but Lara kissed him briefly.

'Goodnight, Tony.'

She walked straight back inside, fighting back tears.

Fran was coming down the stairs.

'That was short and sweet,' she said, her voice softly chiding.

'It was short. What happened to your early night?'

Fran shrugged. 'I wasn't as tired as I thought. I came down to make myself a hot drink.'

'There's half a bottle of wine going off in the fridge.' Lara walked into the kitchen and opened the fridge door. 'It might just run to a glass each.'

It did. Almost. They took it into the sitting-room and Lara switched on the electric fire. It had been chilly all day.

'Tony said he was planning a long weekend with his parents,' Fran told her. 'He said he'd try and travel down to London with me, see me to my flat.'

Lara was pleased. 'I'm glad. You won't feel so bad if Tony's there.'

'No, but what's happened to you and Tony?' she burst out. 'The poor thing looks totally lost and bewildered by it all. And he's gorgeous, Lara.'

Lara raised her eyes to the heavens.

'Everyone's gorgeous as far as you're concerned. Alisdair's gorgeous, Tony's gorgeous.'

'Alisdair *is* gorgeous. He's such good company. But Tony is every girl's dream. He thinks the world of you, too!'

'He does, but — oh, Fran, I've lost count of the nights I spent lying awake, recalling every expression, analysing every word he'd said to try and discover if he loved me or not.'

'Of course he loves you,' Fran retorted.

'No, Fran. He loved Jane. He met Jane and

they were married within six months. He doesn't love me, any more than I love him.'

'Aunt Margaret thinks you're infatuated with Magnus,' Fran said, carefully watching for Lara's reaction.

'I know.'

'And are you?' Fran asked with a disbelieving frown.

'No.'

Fran breathed a sigh of relief. 'That's what I told her. I mean, you hardly know him.'

'I know enough,' Lara answered softly. 'I know he loves me.' She gazed into her cousin's shocked face. 'I don't need to ask him, Fran, and I don't need him to tell me — I just know it.'

'But you and Magnus — '

'I know.'

'But surely — I mean you can't possibly — '

'I know that being loved by Magnus makes me feel very special. It makes everything feel right. And I love being with him. He's so easy to be with.' A sudden smile lit her face. 'And sometimes he's impossible to be with. But easy or impossible, I want to be with him every second of every day.'

Fran's surprise had changed to utter disbelief. 'But you just said — you're surely not trying to tell me that you're in love with him!'

Lara nodded.

Fran took a full minute to accept this.

'I can see the attraction, up to a point,' she said at last, although she sounded full of doubts. 'It's the same with Ally. They're fit, strong and full of energy. It's attractive. And people say the sea makes heroes out of men.'

'And widows out of women.' Lara sighed. 'And that's where it all falls apart. If he worked on shore, he wouldn't be happy and he wouldn't be the same man, would he? But I couldn't live that life.

'Shona wasn't much older than I am now when her husband drowned. I couldn't go through that. I couldn't put my children through what Magnus and Alisdair had to go through. I keep telling myself that there are more people killed on the roads — '

'Only because there are more people using the roads,' Fran said bluntly. 'Let's face it, there aren't many traffic jams in the Atlantic.'

'I know,' Lara agreed. 'And I couldn't live like that. I couldn't listen to the wind, or look at the fog . . . I just couldn't do it.' Her voice held a note of appeal. 'What am I going to do, Fran?'

Fran shook her head in bewilderment. 'Are you quite sure that you're not on the rebound? Are you sure, really sure that you're in love with Magnus?'

Lara swallowed hard. 'Yes. And we can't go on like this. Magnus knows it. I know it. What am I going to do, Fran?'

'No wonder Aunt Margaret's in such a state!'

'She keeps saying 'But he's a fisherman, Lara' as if I hadn't noticed that.' Lara's voice hovered between amusement and exasperation. 'And Shona approves even less.'

'Why?' Fran was surprised.

'I suppose she feels like Mum. I expect she wants something better for her son. I expect she wants a woman who'll sit at home knitting thick sweaters to keep him warm at sea, someone who can cook him wholesome, nourishing meals . . . And that's not me, is it?'

'Hardly.' Fran grinned.

But it wasn't funny. 'I'm going to bed,' Lara announced wearily.

There was no point in spending the night searching for answers, because there were no answers. She couldn't live with him, and she couldn't live without him.

With him. Without him. The words echoed in her mind as she walked up the stairs.

Yet without him was the only possible option. She'd coped without Magnus for the last thirty years — though, for the life of her she couldn't imagine how — so presumably she could cope without him for the next thirty. She had her work, he had the sea . . .

★ ★ ★

The churchyard gate protested with a deafening creak as Lara pushed it open.

'The next time I come,' she told her mother, 'I'm going to bring a can of oil.'

They walked across short, springy grass to the simple headstone bearing the names of Iain James Sutherland and Moira Anne Sutherland.

Margaret gazed at the stone, and then at the faded chrysanthemums.

'These need throwing away.'

'No.' Lara shook her head. 'If Moira could see them, these white chrysanthemums, faded and battered as they are, would mean so much to her. We'll add ours to these.'

Margaret glanced at her sharply, but didn't say anything. Lara was fairly sure she'd guessed who'd brought her mother white chrysanthemums — her father, Anders. But, as usual, she avoided the subject.

Lara knelt down and arranged the flowers among the chrysanthemums.

Iain wouldn't think much to those white flowers, she thought. But he must have accepted that, even if his wife had spent her life loving someone else, and even if the child he'd thought was his was the result of that love — at least he'd had a good wife, a wife who'd stood by him.

'It's always cold here,' Margaret complained. 'The wind goes straight through you.'

'I think it's a beautiful spot.' Lara stood up, drinking in the silence and the peace. The flowers were Lara's way of saying 'I know it's too late, Gran, but I love you.'

But it wasn't too late. It was here that she always sensed Moira's presence — a warm, peaceful, patient presence. She felt it at Braeside, too. In fact, Braeside seemed more Moira's home than Magnus's.

She couldn't share feelings like these with her mother. Margaret would tell her that they arose from within herself — from her need to know that Moira understood. And perhaps they did.

The gate creaked and they both looked towards it. Lara spotted the white chrysanthemums.

'It's Anders.' She clasped her mother's arm and Margaret stiffened.

'No, it isn't,' she said, with a touch of relief, as the distant figure took slow, painful steps towards them.

Not so long ago, Lara thought sadly, Anders had imagined he could walk here from his house. Now, he struggled to complete the short distance from the gate.

Margaret gasped as the realisation hit her. 'I wouldn't have recognised him!'

When Anders reached them, his breathing was laboured and wheezy.

'Has Shona brought you?' Lara asked.

He nodded.

'About time, too!' she teased him. 'These chrysanthemums are well past their best.'

He smiled, taking time to catch his breath.

'They're not the only ones.'

The smile still in place, he turned to Margaret.

'Hello, Meg.'

'Hello. I'm so sorry to hear that you're not well.'

Lara cringed. Margaret's words had been laden with pity. There was no love, no affection even, just pity. And Anders could take anything but that.

He shrugged it off.

'You look well,' he said quietly. 'Robert, too. You must miss Lara, now that she's living here.'

'Very much.'

'She's in safe hands,' Anders assured her gently. 'She's among friends.' She smiled at

Lara briefly. 'I think she belongs here.'

Margaret's reply was stiff. 'It makes a nice change for her and she'd been thinking about general practice for some time. But I can't see it being challenging enough for her in the long run.'

With that said, Margaret spoke quickly of the weather, how it was always cold and windy when she visited, and she spoke briefly of the changes in Lerwick . . .

'Well, Lara,' she said finally, 'it's time we left. Anders will want to be alone.'

Before Lara could gather her wits. Margaret had already turned away.

'Meg!'

Anders' voice, stronger than Lara had heard it, stopped his daughter mid-stride. She turned around, her eyes wary.

'Meg, we won't meet again,' Anders said simply. He sought the right words. 'Moira and I — we made mistakes, but we loved each other. And you — we couldn't have loved you more. The mistakes we made, we made because we loved you. We did what we thought was right for you.

'It wasn't, of course.' He sighed. 'You suffered — we all did. We were a family that was forever divided, and we missed out on so much.

'It's too late for Moira and me now, but it's

220

not too late for you, Meg, or for Lara,' he said urgently. 'Don't let your bitterness keep you away from here — away from Lara. She needs you, just as you need her. Don't let the mistakes Moira and I made come between you.'

Margaret's eyes filled with tears. She took half a step towards him, but stopped again.

'I won't,' she said huskily.

She tried to say something else but couldn't. She turned on her heel and hurried away from them.

Lara was about to follow, but Anders' frail hand on her arm came as a relief. She watched Margaret until she was nothing more than a shape seen through the blur of tears.

'Let me.' She took the flowers from Anders and knelt to put them on the grave. She took her time, removing the old ones and replacing them with perfect white blooms. Every now and then she had to wipe away her tears with the sleeve of her jacket.

When she stood up, the task completed, Anders' gaze was still on the gate.

Lara slipped her arm through his.

Was he right? Was that the last time father and daughter would meet? And if so, how could either of them accept it?

'Don't live the life I've lived, Lara.' Blue-grey eyes suddenly burned into Lara's.

'It can be such a lonely life. And it can be a terribly long one.'

The thought of Magnus clutched at Lara's heart. How could she condemn them both to a life without love?

9

A shaft of early morning sunlight streamed through the window, putting Lara under a spotlight as she knelt on the floor by Anders' chair.

She looked completely free from worry, Magnus thought. He didn't suspect for a moment that she was, but she seemed relaxed and her laughter came easily.

He knew that her parents' visit had upset her. No, that wasn't true. Seeing Robert had brought her nothing but happiness. It was Margaret's visit that had upset her.

Towards the end of their stay, Lara's mother had relaxed and things had been less strained, but Magnus knew that Lara had been hoping for — and expecting — so much more.

Fran and Tony had left together two days ago for London. By all accounts, Lara and her cousin had talked long into the night on several occasions, and Magnus suspected Lara was finding the house a little quite now.

More important than any of that, of course, was Anders. He had good days and bad days, but the bad days were getting worse, and more frequent.

Today was one of the bad days. It was impossible to look at Anders without being reminded that he had very little time left.

'You're looking thoughtful, Magnus,' Anders remarked, and Magnus dragged his gaze from Lara.

'I was just wondering when I might get a word in!'

'We're all ears,' Lara retorted, then she laughed as it became obvious that he had nothing to say.

'Lara,' Anders chided, 'you haven't checked on my medicines today.'

'No,' she replied airily, 'and I'm not going to.' Her expression changed. 'Oh, did you want a cup of tea?'

'Please.' Smiling, Anders nodded.

His troubled gaze followed her as she got to her feet and went into the kitchen.

'Bad night?' Magnus asked quietly.

Anders nodded. 'I just wish,' he said quietly, 'that Lara was half as strong as she pretends to be.'

So did Magnus.

'We haven't had long,' Anders went on, 'and she won't be able to share it with her family. What with Meg and — ' He left the sentence unfinished. 'It will hit her hard.

Magnus,' he said sadly.

'Yes, I know.'

'Take care of her,' Anders said urgently. 'Make her see that although we haven't had long, we've shared something very special. Make her see that quality is far more important than quantity. Make her understand that I don't want it to drag on. Make her remember what we've had and be happy . . .'

The effort left Anders struggling for breath. Magnus leaned forward and put his hand on the old man's arm.

'I'll take care of her, Anders. I promise.'

'Yes.' Anders' concern relaxed into a gentle smile. 'Yes, of course you will, Magnus.'

Satisfied, he slumped back in his chair — but only for a few moments.

'There's something I've been meaning to give you, Magnus,' he said quietly. 'Come and see me tomorrow,' he suggested, nodding in the direction of the kitchen, 'when Lara's at the surgery.'

Before Magnus could comment, Lara came in with a tray.

'You two are looking very serious,' she noticed.

'We've been talking about the Kristiansund Jewel,' Magnus lied, and he caught her quick frown. He wished Anders would forget all

225

about it, too, but worrying about something lost half a century ago had to be better than worrying about how his death would affect his granddaughter.

'I've been trying to put myself in Jakob's place,' he went on. 'Your brother must have risked his own skin, and yours, Anders, by getting to your boat.'

Anders nodded.

'But when he saw you,' Magnus said, 'there was no brotherly chat, was there? If I was seeing Ally for what I thought might be the last time, I'd have far more important things to talk about than how he'd hidden things on his boat. There must have been a very important reason, more important than a final few words with his brother, for Jakob to take such an interest.'

Anders was recalling that last conversation with his brother.

'Such as?'

'I think he was looking for a hiding place. I think he put the shield on *your* boat.'

There was an electric silence as Anders' lively mind considered this.

'It's possible, I suppose. He'd have had the chance. But, no, there was nothing on our boat. One of us would have known.'

His eyes clouded with memories.

'I remember that trip so clearly. We were

lucky to get back to Shetland ourselves. A German plane had spotted us. Luckily, the visibility was bad so it didn't do too much damage. It did enough, though, and we limped back to Shetland, way off course.

'It wasn't the trip, though, so much as what happened when we got back.'

Lara had poured his tea, and she held it for him to sip before Anders went on.

'With the morning light, we could see land but we still weren't sure that we'd make it. Then a local boat spotted us. It was Sam, Moira's father.'

'My great-grandfather!' Lara said, her eyes wide.

'Yes. There was no question that he saved our lives. Then, less than twenty-four hours later, he died of a heart attack.'

'No!' Lara cried. 'Oh, poor Moira. He couldn't have been very old.'

'He wasn't, at least, not in years, but he was all Moira had left. Shortly after Moira got married, her mother went south to stay with her sister in Coventry. Just before the Blitz there. Coventry was devastated.

'I remember Moira telling me she'd wanted to go with her mother. In fact, if she hadn't been one of the many in Shetland who went down with the flu, she would have gone.'

'Poor Moira,' Lara said again.

'Yes, and poor Sam, too,' Anders said with a sigh. 'He never got over it.'

'They lived at Kerlea, didn't they?' Magnus asked.

'That's right,' Anders told him, 'and Sam rented the building — well, it's yours now, isn't it? Part of Braeside?'

Magnus nodded.

'That's where Sam built his boat,' Anders recalled with a smile. 'Anyway, Sam spotted us, and towed our boat, or what was left of it, home.'

Anticipating Magnus' question, he added, 'All we wanted was sleep. The next day, though, we went out to inspect the boat. It was where Sam had left it and there was nothing on it. When it had been repaired, it made more journeys to Norway.'

'Perhaps Sam looked over it first, and moved anything he thought a bit suspicious?' Magnus suggested.

'Why would he do that?' Anders asked.

'I don't know,' Magnus admitted. 'But think of the rumours that must have been flying about the Shetland Bus. He must have been curious.'

'No. After losing his wife, Sam had no interest in anything.'

'But you'd just taken ammunition to Norway,' Magnus persisted. 'Perhaps he was checking to make sure you hadn't brought any back with you. Perhaps he was worried that children might get to it.'

'But supposing Jakob *did* hide it on our boat,' Anders said slowly, 'and supposing Sam *was* curious and *did* find the shield? What would he have done with it?'

Lara and Magnus looked at each other.

'He would have brought it to us,' Anders said. 'Or he would have taken it home for safekeeping. Or he would have taken it to Moira. Either way, if it had been in his possession when he died, Moira would have come across it.' Anders smiled fondly. 'I know Moira could be a little forgetful but I don't think even she could forget something like that.'

'I suppose you're right,' Magnus agreed reluctantly.

He was beginning to realise why Anders couldn't forget about this. It was beginning to pray on his own mind, too. He kept reminding himself that, at first, Anders hadn't even been sure that he'd actually seen Jakob. Now that he was sure, he was only guessing that Jakob's cargo had been the Kristiansund Jewel . . .

Soon afterwards the minister arrived to see Anders.

'We'll call and see you later,' Lara promised

as they were leaving.

As Magnus drove them away, he thought of the day ahead, stretching in front of them like a promise. Lara wasn't working, nor even on call. For the rest of the day, he had her all to himself.

'Why did Anders want me out of the way?' she asked suddenly. 'When he sent me off to make the tea?'

'He wanted a cup of tea!' Magnus caught her knowing glance. 'I don't know — all right, your name might have been mentioned but it was nothing important.'

'I hope he isn't worrying about me,' she said softly. Then, with a catch in her voice, she added briskly, 'Remind him that I'm a doctor, Magnus. Life and death — it's all part and parcel of the job. We're used to it.'

'Lara, don't — '

But she didn't want to hear. 'Where are we going?'

'I've no idea,' he replied. 'Where would you like to go?'

She smiled, as if having the choice was pleasure enough.

'St Ninian's Isle. You can show me the remains of the old church because I've yet to be convinced that they exist.'

'You haven't seen them?' he asked in amazement.

'I haven't *found* them. Fran and I walked miles looking for them.'

'But there's a sign!'

'Pointing straight on,' she told him. 'If you follow that, you end up in the sea. We met a couple of holidaymakers and they hadn't been able to find them, either.'

'Townies!' Magnus said with a exasperated laugh. 'You can't find anything unless it has flashing neon lights above it.'

When he stopped the car, she jumped out and ran down towards the sand. Magnus followed and she stopped to wait for him, wrapping her arms around herself.

'It's freezing,' she said on a laugh. 'Are you sure these remains are worth seeing?'

'Not to be missed.' He hugged her close as they walked.

She laughed, then went to the other side of him so that his body protected her from the wind.

'Do you really think that Jakob might have put the shield on Anders' boat?' she asked.

'I don't know, but why else would he be so interested in where they'd hidden the ammunition? A casual interest, yes, but a man who's convinced he isn't going to see the dawn doesn't take a casual interest in anything, does he?'

'It would mean everything to Anders, if we

could find out what happened to it,' Lara said with feeling.

'I know, but I don't think we ever will. It could still be in Norway, or in Shetland, I suppose. It could be at the bottom of the sea somewhere in between. It could be in Germany . . .'

They reached what was left of the 12th-century church, where the Pictish silver had been found in the late Fifties.

'Fran and I were looking for something — taller,' Lara said with amusement.

However, she had satisfied her curiosity and they walked back along the sand.

Magnus suddenly wondered if Margaret was right. When Anders was gone, would there be anything to keep Lara in Shetland? Her work perhaps but, after so long in a busy hospital, would that be enough?

Breakers were crashing in on their right, while on their left, the water gently lapped against the sand. There wasn't a soul in sight. Lara's hand was clasped tightly in his as she made patterns in the sand with her shoes.

'I feel as if I'm on holiday.' She laughed happily. 'No work, no visitors, no telephones. Just the sea and the sky and the sand — and you.'

And you. His heart leapt. She turned as

232

she said that and Magnus captured her face in his hands.

Their kiss was gentle at first. He could taste the salt of the sea breeze on her lips. He could feel her fingers tangling themselves in his hair.

Then the kiss deepened. The tighter she held him, the more his sense of longing threatened to overwhelm him.

When he finally looked into her face, the sun had caught her hair, making it shine like polished silver. Her lips were trembling, and in her eyes, he swore he saw all the love he felt for her reflected back.

'Marry me,' he said huskily.

'No!' She struggled away from him.

His words had been more of a longing spoken aloud than a question, but her 'no' had come with all the force of a bullet from a gun.

He took a step towards her but she took a step back. There was nothing in her eyes now, nothing but accusation.

'No,' she said again, slightly more calmly, 'I won't marry you, Magnus. You know it wouldn't work. How can you even ask? You need a wife who — '

'I need *you*, Lara.'

'No!' She screamed the word at him. 'I couldn't make you happy, surely you can see

233

that. I'd be a nervous wreck if I had to spend my days wondering when you'd come back, or *if* you'd come back.'

'Lara,' Magnus said calmly, 'there are eighty-year-old men living here who've spent their whole lives at sea.'

'I know that.'

'Something might happen to me,' he went on carefully, 'just as something might happen to you. But every time I'm away, you convince yourself that I won't come back. That's ridiculous. I will come back, Lara.'

'Robbie didn't come back,' she cried.

It always came back to that. No matter how many times he tried to make her see sense, she always reminded him that his father hadn't come back.

'Remember what that was like, Magnus. I've spoken to Shona, and I know what it did to you. At fourteen you took responsibility for Shona and Ally, and you couldn't cope with any of it. You didn't cry, you didn't talk to anyone, you lost your friends, you almost got thrown out of school . . . Well, I'm damned if I'll put my children through that.'

'You're wrong, darling. I cried every night.'

His days had been spent listening to people telling him that time healed, that his dad had gone to a better place, that each day it would hurt a little less . . .

He'd bullied Ally into doing homework. He'd made sure that Shona ate something, no matter how little. Then, when night came, and another day had been survived, he'd crept out of the house and down to the shore. There, in a fury of grief and rage, he had shouted and screamed at the heavens. Then he had wept . . .

'Tell me you don't love me,' he said.

Her head snapped up in surprise. Then she gave a careless shrug.

'I don't love you, Magnus.'

He didn't believe her, but it still hurt that she could say it so easily.

They stood with a yard of sand between them. A herring gull hovered for a moment, as if it too was waiting. Even the waves seemed to be holding back, waiting.

'Promise me you won't ask again,' Lara said at last.

Magnus shook his head. 'I can't do that, Lara. I love you.'

She closed her eyes.

'I suppose that's it then,' she said quietly. 'We can't carry on with that hanging over us. It wouldn't be fair to you — or to me. I suppose I've always known that it couldn't —

'I've been selfish, Magnus. I like being with you, and when I look back on all the special days, you've always been there.

'And then I've thought of Anders. I thought that if you were with me when he died, it wouldn't be quite so hard . . .

'People think that because I'm a doctor — I know I've just told you, I'm a doctor, I can cope. But with Anders — '

Her bottom lip quivered and she bit it hard.

'People don't think that,' Magnus said gently.

'They do,' she insisted. 'They think it's easier. They're wrong. If anything, it's harder. I've seen Tony in tears over someone he'd only met a few hours before. You see too much of it. It can be the most hateful job — But you do it. If you can ease just one person's suffering, if you can save just one life, then it's all worthwhile. But with Anders — '

Tears spilled onto her cheeks.

'With Anders I can't do anything. Nobody can. All anyone can do is sit back and watch him die. I thought — it was selfish, I know — but I thought that if you were with me, it wouldn't be quite so unbearable.

'Sometimes, I can force myself to forget. But seeing him today, it hit me all over again. It was just like — '

She couldn't go on. She crumpled before him, until she was kneeling on the sand, her hands covering her face as she gave in to her tears. Magnus knelt beside her.

'I know, Lara,' he said softly. 'I felt exactly the same. But it *will* be bearable. And I *will* be with you.'

'You won't, Magnus.'

'I will!' Even as he spoke, he knew he wouldn't, because she wouldn't allow it.

Magnus thanked God that Anders couldn't see her now. The sight of her would break Anders' heart, just as it was breaking his own.

'I won't ask again, Lara.' His voice was hoarse.

She raised her tear-wet face.

'I won't ask you to marry me again, Lara. I promise.'

For a second, he thought it wasn't enough, but very slowly, she moved into his arms and buried her face against him. As the tears continued to flow, Magnus held her as if she were a small child.

Two promises in one day. And both were rash, and impossible to keep . . .

★ ★ ★

Lara had just got home and switched on the television to catch the news when she heard her door open.

237

'Camerons' Delivery Service!' a cheerful voice called.

Smiling, she went into the kitchen. Alisdair was putting a large cardboard box on her table.

'What's that?'

'Mum's been baking, and there was a slight miscalculation. Our freezer's full, Magnus' is full — There's a batch ready to take to Anders in the morning. Mum thought you might have space.'

'The dear woman!' Lara peered into the box. 'I've always got space in my freezer. I'll ring and thank her. I was going to call on her tomorrow anyway.'

'Lara?' Alisdair perched himself on the edge of her table.

'Yes?'

'Do you think you could have a word with Mum? See if there's anything bothering her?'

There was no 'if', Lara thought. Something was definitely bothering Shona. She had assumed that it was too much worrying about Magnus and Alisdair but now she was beginning to suspect there was something more.

'I'll try,' she replied, 'but I asked her before and she — '

'I can imagine,' Alisdair interrupted. 'I've been snapped at a few times myself. Mum worries about the world and his wife but no one's allowed to worry about her.

'There's something wrong though,' he went on. 'Yesterday, she spent most of the day reading a book. She reads magazines, yes. She tries out the recipes and knitting patterns. She reads an article and then puts it aside for a day. But I can't remember the last time she sat down and read a book.

'Then today,' he explained, 'there was this frenzy of baking. It was so unnecessary!'

'I'll have a word with her tomorrow,' Lara promised.

'Thanks, Lara.'

His cheerful smile was back in place, which reminded her of something else.

'Ally, can I ask you a personal question?'

'If I can ask you one,' he replied immediately.

'Deal.' She laughed.

'Well?' he prompted as she hesitated.

'It's about Anna Thompson,' she said.

That clearly shook him.

'I was being nosy,' Lara admitted, 'and Magnus told me that there was once something between you and Anna.'

'That was years ago,' Alisdair said in amazement. His expression altered. 'She's not — seriously ill, is she?'

'She's going to be fine,' Lara assured him

quickly. 'She's taken a lot of knocks but she'll be fine. Really.'

It was true. Lara had had complete faith in the counsellor helping Anna, but even she'd been amazed by the improvement. It hadn't only been James, though. It had been Anna, too. She'd had to pluck up courage to admit to people — people like Shona who would be willing to look after Rachel for a few hours — that she was an outpatient at the hospital. And much to Anna's surprise, she'd met with nothing but offers of help.

Lara and her patient had become good friends by now. Her visits rarely had a professional reason behind them nowadays. Anna was becoming good company.

'She needs a friend, Ally,' Lara remarked.

Alisdair laughed, a short laugh that had little, if any, humour in it.

'I don't think I'm the ideal candidate.'

'You know Rachel's just getting over measles?'

'Yes. Mum told me.'

'She'd be pleased to see you,' Lara pointed out carefully.

'Rachel would, yes. But Anna — '

'What happened?' Lara asked.

He expelled his breath on a sigh. 'As Magnus said, it was a long time ago. It didn't last long, either. Six weeks and four days, to be precise,' he added with a rueful smile.

Lara smiled at him. 'That's very precise.'

'Everything was great, till one night, there was a dance on, and at the last minute, Anna couldn't go for some reason. So I went on my own. Then she found that she could go and she decided to surprise me.' His gaze held Lara's. 'When she arrived, I was kissing someone else.'

'Oh, Ally! You're incorrigible.' Lara laughed.

'Anna was seventeen, and I was twenty. But that's no excuse, is it? I suppose it was a case of not realising what I had until I lost it.'

Anna certainly knew how to pick them, Lara thought.

'I still say she needs a friend,' she told Alisdair. 'What happened was a long time ago and it's best forgotten. Anyway, Anna's not the type to bear a grudge. Why not call and see her sometime?'

'Why me?' he asked with a puzzled frown.

'Because I've seen you with Rachel,' Lara answered thoughtfully, 'and because I've seen you with other people. No matter how low a person's feeling, you always manage to make them smile. That's rare gift to have. You should put it to good use.'

As an afterthought, she added quickly. 'But

she needs friends. And only friends. Nothing more.'

'I should be so lucky,' Alisdair said dryly.

She laughed softly. 'You'll go and see her?'

'I'll go and see Rachel.'

Lara was satisfied. She had no worries about Anna falling for Alisdair again. He'd earned himself a reputation since his twenties.

For all that, Alisdair was a highly loveable rogue and a good friend to have. She'd thought many times that Alisdair's sunny nature and sense of humour ought to be available on prescription.

'Right, my turn with the personal questions.' Alisdair's eyes were serious, and for some reason, Lara held her breath.

'What have you done to my big brother? He's not happy, Lara.'

Lara wasn't happy either. Three weeks had passed since that awful day when they'd visited St Ninian's Isle.

If he'd chosen any other day to propose, any other time . . . given different circumstances, she would have handled it far more sensibly.

On that day though, she'd been feeling anything but sensible. For days, Anders had looked as if there was enough time left but that day, Lara had been forced to face up to the fact that they had hardly any time left at all. Only years of training had helped her keep a smile on her face.

She'd done her best to forget everything about the day; Anders' appearance, the way she'd broken down on the sand. It was impossible but she'd tried.

Fool that she was, she'd hoped that she and Magnus could carry on as before but, of course, they couldn't.

They still saw quite a lot of each other and, if Magnus was home, they visited Anders together, but things were strained to say the least.

They'd seen Anders that very morning. Lara had reached across Magnus for something, and had put her hand on his shoulder to save herself from over-balancing. He'd flinched as if her touch had burnt him.

'He'll get over it, Ally.'

Alisdair gazed into her troubled face.

'And will you get over it, too?'

'Of course,' she replied quickly. 'Given time, people get over anything.'

'Hmm,' Alisdair murmured doubtfully. 'Well, it wasn't much of an answer but I can see it's all I'm going to get. If ever you need a shoulder — '

'I'll bear you in mind.' Lara hugged him briefly.

★ ★ ★

Tony was standing in the hospital's reception area, talking on the phone, when Lara walked in. He was surprised she'd heard so soon, though, of course, news travelled fast in Shetland.

She didn't see him, but as soon as he'd finished his call, he went over to her.

A sudden smile lit her face, and Tony had a sneaking suspicion that she hadn't heard, after all.

'Have you got a spare bed?' she asked with a smile. 'Or just a quiet corner where I can curl up and sleep? Remember when we went for days with sleep being nothing more than a memory? Well, I was called out three times last night and I feel awful. I suppose it's age catching up with me.'

Tony's heart sank. She obviously hadn't heard, but the expression on his face had alerted her.

'What's wrong, Tony?'

'Probably nothing,' he said, 'but we're on standby. We had a call from the Coastguard.'

Lara's hand clenched and flew to her mouth, as if that were the only way she could stop herself from crying out. A whole host of emotions flashed across her face then she laid her hand against her chest.

244

'What's happened?' Her voice was barely a whisper.

'I don't know any details, Lara, but there's been a fire on the *Ermingerd*.'

'A fire?' She looked about her wildly, at the main doors, at the reception desk, at the floor, at the clock on the wall. Tony knew the feeling. She longed to do something, but there was nothing she could do.

'I expect it's all under control,' Tony tried to reassure her. 'We're often put on standby. It's routine, you know it is. And Magnus knows what he's doing. Everyone says he's one of the best.'

'Yes, everyone says that,' she agreed wildly, 'and they probably say it about everyone else. They probably said it about his father. But even Magnus can't walk on water, can he?' She ran her fingers through her hair.

'I'm sorry, Tony. I didn't mean to snap.'

'I know, love. I just meant that he knows what he's doing,' Tony said gently.

'Yes.'

Tony could see that the knowledge was of no consolation whatsoever.

'Have you seen what the weather's like out there?' she asked shakily, and he nodded. The wind was ferocious, bringing with it furious bursts of hail and rain.

If he'd had any doubts about her feelings

for Magnus, the terror in her eyes now dispelled them all. Deep down, there hadn't been any doubts though. Lara and Magnus might be an unlikely couple but that didn't stop Lara loving him.

To outsiders, he and Jane had been an equally unsuited couple. But he'd loved her to distraction.

He knew now that Lara had been right. He loved Lara, he truly did, but not in the way he'd loved Jane. Never in that way.

The day he learned that Jane was dead, he'd wanted to die, too. The thought of Lara having to go through that was unbearable.

10

That morning seemed endless. Lara made four calls, keeping her mind on the job by a heroic effort, and then decided to call on Anna Thompson.

Lara reminded herself that whatever had happened or was happening on the *Ermingerd*, there was nothing she could do.

Anna's radio was tuned to the local station and she'd clearly heard about the *Ermingerd*. She couldn't say so, though, because young Rachel, her daughter, was in the kitchen, cuddling her beloved bear.

'Can you stay for lunch?' Anna asked.

The thought of food sickened her. 'Thanks, but no. I've got too much to do.'

Rachel held out her bear.

'Alisdair gave me this when I was ill,' she said, when Lara stroked him. 'I'm going to marry Ally, you know.'

'Yes, I know.' Lara grinned at her, but Rachel's mother looked anxious.

'Rachel's obsessed with marriage,' Anna said worriedly. 'Do you think that's because I'm *not* married?'

'No. Every five-year-old girl has decided on

her future husband. I was going to marry the man who ran the corner shop — probably because he gave me a chocolate bar every time he saw me. I think he reached retirement age when I was seven.'

'I suppose you're right.' Anna laughed.

'Of course I am. Besides, all the girls fall for Alisdair. And rightly, too. He has a heart of pure gold and I'd trust him with my life.'

'Oh, so would I,' Anna agreed dryly. 'I'd even trust him with my daughter. But I wouldn't trust him with my heart.'

'Well, no.'

But Lara couldn't bear to think of Alisdair's heart of gold or that carefree smile of his — or Magnus.

When she left Anna's, Lara drove straight home. She switched on the radio but there was no news, and even if there had been it wasn't necessarily up to date.

She tried Magnus' number. It rang and rang. Several times she tried to replace the receiver, but imagined him walking into the house.

No wonder Shona wore a permanent expression of worry. To have lost a husband to the sea, to have both sons on one boat . . .

She called Shona. 'It's me — Lara. Do you want me to come over?'

'Oh, Lara.' Shona sounded weary. 'It's

kind, my dear, but — do you mind if I say no? We can't really help each other . . . '

'No, I understand.' Lara swallowed. 'You'll let me know, Shona, if — '

'Yes. When they get in touch, we'll ring each other,' Shona said firmly.

'Whoever hears first.'

She rang off, and Lara went upstairs and lay on her bed.

She'd been lying there for an hour, refusing to acknowledge that the already strong wind was strengthening by the minute, when she heard a vehicle stop outside.

She leapt off the bed to look out of the window, and sagged with relief when she saw Magnus's Land Rover. She raced down the stairs and ran to open the door. But it wasn't Magnus. She felt the blood drain away, heard a roaring sound in her ears . . .

'Lara? Hey, Lara? Are you OK?'

A voice penetrated the fog, and Lara stared at Ivan, one of the *Ermingerd's* crew.

'We had a problem with the *Ermingerd*,' he explained with a curious frown. 'I was passing — thought I'd let you know that Magnus would be delayed. Lara? Are you ill?'

She shook her head, partly to reassure Ivan that she wasn't ill and partly to fight off the nausea. 'Magnus is all right?'

Still frowning, Ivan nodded. 'Of course.'

Lara looked at the Land Rover, then back at Ivan.

'Oh, no — I had a lift to the boat with Magnus,' he explained quickly, 'so I'm taking the Land Rover home. I'll get Marie to follow me back so that I can leave it for him at the quay.'

'Why aren't you on the boat?'

'They always get the crew off if there's a problem.' He shrugged. 'The skipper and mate stay on board.'

'Magnus and Alisdair?'

'Yes.'

'I saw — ' Lara cleared her throat. 'I saw Tony at the hospital. He said there was a fire.'

'Aye, in the engine room. We lost power and electrics, and ran onto rocks.'

'Why are Magnus and Alisdair still on board?'

'They're going to try and refloat her. We got the power back and she's upright on the rocks.'

'And if they can't?'

'Then they can't,' he said carelessly. 'But they've got a couple of lines aboard. They'll be OK.'

'I see. Well, thanks for — '

Ivan put his hand on hers. 'There's nothing to worry about,' he said quietly. 'She'll be escorted home, and if there's any damage,

250

they'll soon know about it.'

'Yes. Thanks for stopping by, Ivan. You'd better go before Marie starts worrying.'

'Come with me,' he suggested. 'Marie would love to see you.'

Lara gave him a smile, a professional one courtesy of years of training.

'Thanks, Ivan, but I can't. I've got a million things to do before tonight's surgery. I'll just give Shona a call, and then get started.'

'You're OK?' he asked doubtfully.

The smile remained in place. 'Fine, thanks . . .'

The moment he'd driven off, Lara's shoulders sagged. She shuddered, and burst into racking sobs.

★ ★ ★

After the evening surgery, Lara paid her grandfather a visit. She'd hoped to be able to tell him that Magnus and Alisdair were home, but it hadn't worked out that way.

'You look worn out,' Anders said with concern.

'Bad night.' She called up a smile. 'I was called out three times. Nothing serious, thank goodness, but I'll be glad to get some sleep.'

He accepted that. 'Sit, sit. Look, the tea's made. We'll talk, shall we?'

Lara leaned her head back and nodded wearily.

'Do you know,' he said, 'the more I think about it, the more I think Magnus might be right.'

'About what?' Her head came up at once.

'The Kristiansund Jewel.'

Not that again! Lara groaned inwardly.

Her nerves were in shreds and all the while Ivan's words went round and round in her mind — *force nines, swells of thirty feet or more, seas that would kill a man in minutes.*

'Jakob *might* have put it on our boat,' Anders went on.

'Perhaps he did.' Lara reached for the teapot and began to pour out.

'Magnus isn't home yet then?'

'Not as far as I know.' Lara avoided his gaze.

Anders gave her a searching look.

'Worrying won't bring him home any quicker. Be patient, Lara. Magnus is — '

'Don't!' she cut him off. 'If anyone else tells me he's one of the best, I shall probably scream!'

'But he is.' He smiled.

'What makes him better than anyone else?' she scoffed.

'Probably all the things that infuriate his crew! There's no need to worry if there are enough life-jackets on board the *Ermingerd*, or if they've been lent out to someone and forgotten about, because Magnus will have checked. There's no need to worry if the radios are working. He'll have had them checked and double-checked.

'His crew say he's over-cautious, and perhaps he is. When you first arrived here, they were hardly going out at all and, when they did go out, they didn't go far. They'd had some work done on a generator and he wasn't happy about it. As it turned out he was right, but he wasn't popular with the crew. He was costing them a lot of money. Unless he's one hundred per cent confident, he won't take her out.'

'But accidents happen,' Lara insisted.

'Of course they do,' Anders agreed. 'Boats break down just as cars do.'

'There's a slight difference!'

'Not really. If your car breaks down, you do what it takes to get it going again. If the *Ermingerd* breaks down, Magnus does whatever it takes.'

Seeing that she wasn't reassured, Anders went on, 'It's hard for you to understand, Lara. If you were out there, you'd be frightened, but Magnus won't be. It's a way of life to him.' He thought for a moment.

'Although there was a time, I think, when

the sea did frighten him. As a child, he spent every minute he could on the water. But when his father died — Well, I can't say for certain that it was fear, but Robbie died in June and Magnus didn't go on the water until the following November.'

Magnus had never mentioned that to her.

'And when he did go — ' Anders shook his head. 'He took his father's boat out on a cruel November night. It was one of the worst storms we'd seen for years. We'd been out in worse during the war, of course, but in wartime you did things that would have been suicidal in normal times. And what Magnus did that night seemed little short of suicidal. The *Merlin* wasn't up to it, and Magnus, at fourteen, certainly wasn't.

'Shona was beside herself,' Anders recalled. 'I can still remember sitting with her on that long night. Eventually, in walked Magnus with not a word to anyone. To this day, I don't know if it was fear that took him out that night, or temper — or what it was.'

'Sheer recklessness?' Lara shuddered.

Anders smiled. 'Oh, certainly that, but he was just a child. Whatever the reason. though, it did him good. After that, he seemed more able to accept things, more able to cope. And it was the last risk he ever took.'

'Is he really so good?' Lara desperately

needed convincing.

'Yes.' Anders didn't hesitate.

'And his father — was he as good?'

'No.'

'What about Alisdair?'

Anders smiled.

'Alisdair could be, but — no, without Magnus pushing him, he'd let things slip.'

Her grandfather leaned back in his chair and closed his eyes.

'I'd better go,' Lara said quietly, 'you're tired. How have you been?'

He made a dismissive gesture with one hand.

'As well as can be expected, I believe would be the term you medical lot would use.'

His eyes twinkled at her. 'Where are you off to?'

She'd been going home but now — 'Perhaps I'll go to Braeside and wait for Magnus.'

Anders nodded with satisfaction.

'Good idea. And just remember, Lara, there's a power out there that's far greater than the sea. God decides who comes home safe from the sea, not the sea.'

Tears sprang to Lara's eyes, and she hugged Anders. 'I wish I was as wise as you.'

'At your age, I wasn't very wise, was I? Unfortunately, few of us are granted wisdom until it's too late to put it to good use.

Although,' he added, giving her a knowing glance, 'I was wise enough to tell Moira how I felt.'

Lara flushed.

'Have faith,' Anders whispered. 'He'll be home soon.'

★　★　★

Magnus drove round the corner into sight of his home. The lights were on — all of them. The place lit the night sky like a beacon.

He wasn't too surprised to see Lara's car parked next to his own. A little unnerved perhaps but not surprised. He killed the engine but made no attempt to get out of the Land Rover.

If anyone had asked him yesterday what he and Lara had, he would have said nothing. But if he was home, they saw each other every day. They visited Anders together. They had meals together sometimes . . .

It might not be much but it was better than nothing. And he didn't intend to lose it.

Taking a deep breath, and deciding that the best thing was to shrug it off as if nothing had happened, he got out of the Land Rover and walked to the house. He opened the door, very quietly, stepped inside and closed it.

Nothing happened.

He checked the kitchen, then the study, and finally found her in the sitting-room. She was curled up in his chair, with her knees touching her chin, and she was wearing jeans and a blue sweater that he hadn't seen her in before. And, much to his amazement, she was fast asleep.

The house felt cold. He went into the hall, switched on the heating and immediately wished he hadn't. The boiler roared into life, and every radiator in the house started ticking until it sounded as if a dozen bombs were about to explode.

He crept back and saw that she was still asleep.

He stood for several minutes, not daring to breathe, but she didn't stir. Then, he remembered what Marie, Ivan's wife, had told him — he looked like something the cat had dragged ashore — and he tip-toed out of the room and up the stairs.

When he got back from his shave and shower, she was still sleeping. He sat on the chair opposite her.

He wasn't looking forward to this talk. Lara would remind him that his father had died at sea. He would remind her that thousands of men *hadn't* died at sea . . . he dreaded it, and what was the point?

She'd refused to marry him — what

more could he do?

He sat for an hour, watching her. His eyelids were feeling heavy and, given different circumstances, he could have slept, too ... but then, in an instant, she was wide awake. That was when he recognised the sweater she was wearing. It was one of his own.

He knew he was scowling, but there was nothing he could do about it. He wanted to say something casual, to give her a normal greeting, but no words came.

'Are you all right?' she asked.

'Yes!'

The abrupt answer shook her as much as it did him.

'Yes,' he said again, more evenly, 'yes. I'm fine, thanks. It was nothing.'

'What happened?'

'A pipe burst in the engine room,' he explained casually, 'and the water hit the fuse box.'

'I see,' she said quietly, and he knew she didn't see at all.

'Magnus?'

He risked a look at her.

'Yes?'

'Do you still want to marry me?'

The question stunned him. He sat there staring at her, his feelings in turmoil, thoughts racing through his mind.

'I love you, Magnus.'

'You loved me weeks ago, Lara! Nothing's changed. You can't let what happened today — there was never any danger. What did you imagine? The *Ermingerd* engulfed in flames? The crew with third degree burns?'

She wouldn't meet his gaze, and he knew she had imagined exactly that.

'The fire was out in minutes, even before I radioed the Coastguard. It was unfortunate that we lost power and even more unfortunate that while we were trying to restore it, we were heading for the rocks. But it was never dangerous.'

She gazed back at him doubtfully.

'I've thought about giving up the sea, Lara,' he added quietly, 'I've thought of nothing else lately, but what would I do? You see, it's not a case of something I do, it's more a case of something I am.'

'I know that.'

'And I'm not like you. You couldn't pick me up and drop me in the middle of London. I'd be like — '

Words failed him.

'A fish out of water?' Lara suggested dryly.

'Something like that, yes. I was born here and, God willing, I'll die here.'

'I know that, too.' She sounded very subdued.

'Today's been a bad day, Lara, but how will you feel in the morning? Panic has never been a good reason for marriage.'

She stood up.

'I shouldn't have come. It's late. You've had a bad day, I've had a bad day. I expect we're both overwrought. Perhaps I'll see you tomorrow.'

'Lara, stay!' It might have been an instruction to a well-trained dog and he added an apologetic, 'Please.'

She gazed back at him, looking more tired than he'd ever seen her, then finally she sat down again, beside him on the sofa. Slowly, the silence became more comfortable, he reached for her hand and felt her fingers curl around his.

'You're right, Magnus,' she said softly. 'When it comes to the sea my imagination knows no limits. I hate the sea as much as you love it. Within five minutes of hearing about the fire, I was convinced I'd never see you again. Then Ivan gave me a fright. I thought he'd come to tell me you were — '

She shuddered. 'I put off visiting Anders until as late as possible, because I wanted to reassure him that you were home. I didn't want him worrying.'

Magnus smiled at that.

'Anders wouldn't have been worrying.'

'No, he wasn't.' She turned to look at him. 'He told me about the night you took your father's boat out, when you were fourteen.'

'Oh, that. I was just a kid,' he tried to dismiss that.

'Anders said he didn't know if it was fear or anger that made you do it. Which was it?'

'I don't know,' he admitted slowly. 'It was sheer madness, I know that. The *Merlin* hadn't been built for conditions like that, and I'd never been out in anything like it — certainly not on my own.

'I don't know,' he said again. 'Until then, I'd always known that I loved my father. I loved the sea and, when I grew up, I'd spend my life at sea. Then — everything changed. My father was gone, I hated the sea — but I still believed I'd spend my life at sea. It was all I was prepared for.

'I suppose part of it was to convince myself I *wasn't* frightened, and part of it was defiance. My way of telling the sea that I could take anything it threw at me and beat it.

'It was a terrible storm,' he remembered. 'Any one of the waves could have taken me and the *Merlin* with it. I don't think I've been so terrified, or so lonely, in my life. It taught

261

me, though, that when you don't know what you're doing, and when you're on a small boat, the sea will win every time. It's bound to.

'It was strange, but once I'd realised that, I felt quite calm. Life seemed to have a purpose again, even if it was simply getting safely back to dry land.

'Then the storm blew itself out and everything was still. It was eerie. And then I saw the Merry Dancers.'

Lara turned her head, leaning against his shoulder, to look up at him. 'What are they?'

'The Northern Lights.'

'Really? I've never seen them.'

'Never?' he asked in amazement.

She shook her head.

'You will,' he assured her, 'although whether you'll see them as I saw them that night . . . the whole sky was awash with colours — reds, greens, purples — it was amazing. It made me see just how insignificant I was in the grand scale of things. The power out there that night was awesome.'

'Anders said something like that,' Lara told him. 'Actually, he said a lot of things. He even managed to convince me that you were good at your job.'

'I am.' Magnus smiled.

'He also said you drive the crew mad.'

'True, but so long as I'm skipper, they're my responsibility. If they don't like it, there are always other boats.'

'But it was something else Anders said that made me see things more clearly,' she added softly. 'He said that if your number's called, there's nothing you can do about it. He said God decides that, not the sea.'

Magnus smiled, and kissed her hair.

'I'm sure he's right, up to a point. Ally's motto is 'all eyes forward and trust in the Lord'. While I'm a great believer in the power of prayer, I also believe that something more practical doesn't go amiss.'

She smiled at that, and then buried her face against him. He wrapped his arms around her and, moments later, realised she was crying.

'Lara?' he whispered.

'Oh, Magnus — ' Her words were muffled against his chest. 'I want you and I want your children — more than I have ever wanted anything in my life.'

Her words went straight to his heart, and he couldn't speak.

She lifted her tear-stained face. 'Do you still want to marry me?'

'You know I do.'

'You didn't seem very sure.'

'I've been sure for a long time, Lara. I

didn't want it to be a panic reaction. I couldn't bear to think of you regretting it in the morning. You had to be sure.'

'I am sure!'

'Yes, I know.'

He kissed her, tasting the salty tears on her lips. Her kiss was filled with warmth, tenderness — and commitment.

'I love you,' he whispered reverently. He could feel her heart racing in time to his own. In his arms, he held the whole world — the moon, the sun and the stars — and the Merry Dancers, too.

Later, he left her for a moment, and came back carrying a small box.

'Anders gave me this. It's something Moira would never accept from him . . . '

'The ring he wanted to put on her finger?' Lara's eyes shone.

'Yes. He gave it to me. Though it was never on Moira's finger, he wanted it to be on their granddaughter's.'

'Poor Anders,' she said softly. 'It belonged to his mother, you know.'

'Yes, he told me.'

Magnus opened the box, and they gazed at the ring, a blazing ruby guarded by a circle of diamonds. She raised her face, but Magnus doubted if she could see him through her tears.

He drew her close, and she clung to him for a moment.

'You don't have to wear it, darling. You can wear something you've chosen yourself — anything.'

'It's beautiful. Perfect.' She gave him a searching look. 'Unless you'd rather — '

'No.' He brushed away her tears with a gentle finger. 'Wear it for your grandparents. Without them you wouldn't be here — and I wouldn't be the person I am today.'

He slipped the ring on to her finger, and they looked at each other in wonder.

'It might have been made for you,' he said huskily.

'Anders will be so happy.' There was a catch in her voice.

'Smug might be more apt . . . He told me he'd known from the first that we were born for each other. And he couldn't understand why I — I, mind you — was shilly-shallying. And he added that if you'd already had a husband there might — just might — be some excuse!'

She laughed, and snuggled herself close against him. At last they could laugh about the long agonising hours, days and weeks of being unable to exchange a single glance that wasn't painful . . .

Lara's radio-pager bleeped into life, catching her unawares. 'What the — ' Realisation dawned. 'Oh, no. Magnus, I'm on call!'

Magnus glanced at his watch.

'It's two in the morning,' he muttered, and she laughed as she reached for the phone.

'A very popular time for being ill.'

Seconds later, she was on her feet, checking her pocket for her car keys.

'I've got to go.'

Magnus followed her to the door. There still seemed so much to say, so many plans to make.

'You'll come back here?'

'Yes.' She kissed him briefly. 'But I might be late . . . '

* * *

The hospital clock showed ten to five.

Ella Briggs had suffered a mild stroke. Now she was comfortable and, more importantly, reassured. A reassuring word, Lara knew, was often more effective than all the technology in the world.

Lara was tired, but immensely satisfied, and she'd never been happier in her life.

She'd never reconcile herself to Magnus being away at sea, but for the privilege of knowing such complete and utter joy, there had to be a price to pay.

Her footsteps echoed in the quiet corridors. She knew Tony was around because she'd caught a brief glimpse of him earlier. She'd almost given up when he came out of a small room to her side.

'Another busy night?' he asked.

'Just the one call. Actually, I was looking for you, Tony. Are you busy? Can I have a word with you?'

'Of course.' He pushed open a door nearby, and they went inside.

She turned to face him, but suddenly the words wouldn't come.

'Ah,' he said quietly, 'I gather congratulations are in order.'

'How did you know?' Her eyes widened.

He gestured to her left hand. 'You seem to be carrying half the Crown Jewels around with you.'

'Oh!' She laughed, and glanced down at the ring.

'I'm happy for you, Lara. Truly, I am.' He held her hands, but he didn't look very happy. 'It was inevitable, I suppose.' he added. 'The two of you have something very special.'

'Yes, we do.'

'So when's the big day?'

'I don't know,' Lara admitted. 'We haven't had a chance to think about it.'

'I can't imagine Magnus being very patient.'

'Neither can I.' She laughed softly.

He hugged her and kissed the top of her head.

'Tell Magnus from me that he's the luckiest man alive.'

She'd wanted to tell Tony straightaway, before he could hear from anyone else, but it had been much harder than she'd realised. It seemed a crime to wear her happiness so freely and expect everyone to share in it with her.

'Although why anyone in their right mind would want to marry a doctor is beyond me,' Tony added lightly. 'The hours are appalling, the pay's pitiful, the holidays are non-existent . . .'

'And you wouldn't be anything else,' she retorted with a laugh.

'Maybe,' he replied.

The lack of conviction surprised Lara but she guessed that, despite the kind words, he wasn't feeling his best.

Her voice softened. 'Tony — thanks.'

He understood.

'I'll be expecting an invitation, Lara.'

'Of course,' she promised.

★ ★ ★

It was after six when Magnus heard Lara's car return. He had the front door open before she reached it. She was smiling, but she looked like a sleepwalker.

'Everything OK?' he asked.

She walked straight into his arms and buried her face against him.

'Yes. Everything's fine.'

'You need some sleep.'

'No. I need the strongest cup of coffee you have ever seen. I have to be at the surgery in a couple of hours and if I sleep now, I'll feel even worse.' She looked up and smiled at his concern. 'I'm all right, Magnus. Compared to what I used to do at the hospital, this is a holiday.'

'You go and sit down.' He believed her but he still didn't like it. 'I'll make some coffee.'

'Strong coffee.' She yawned.

When he carried it into the sitting room, he thought she was asleep, and sat down opposite her.

She opened her eyes and smiled. 'Tony told me to tell you that you're the luckiest man alive.'

'Does he imagine I don't know that?'

'He also said that you must be mad to marry a doctor.'

A reluctant laugh escaped him. 'Aye, well, I'm inclined to agree with him there.'

She gave a contented sigh and then got out of her chair and knelt on the floor beside him. He'd seen it so many times, and it never failed to amuse him. No matter how many chairs were in a room, she always ended up sitting on the floor.

'When do you want to get married?' she asked sleepily.

'Today. When do you want to get married?'

'Today. But the minister will want to make sure that no one knows of any cause or just impediment.' She smiled at him.

'I expect your mother knows of a dozen.' he warned.

'Only a dozen?'

'She'll try to change your mind.'

'Probably, but she won't succeed.' Lara lifted her head. 'I would rather have one day with you than a lifetime with anyone else.'

She clutched at his hand. 'Magnus, I don't want a honeymoon. I can't go away, not with Anders . . . ' Her voice trailed away.

'We'll postpone it,' Magnus promised. 'We've got the rest of our lives, darling.'

The rest of their lives. He could see in her eyes that same sense of wonder.

'I'll take you on a cruise.' He leaned forward and kissed her, and she spluttered with laughter.

'You will not!'

With a sound that was almost a purr, she rested her head on his leg.

'I'd like to go to Norway . . . to see the fjords . . . to see the waterfalls . . . '

'Then we'll go to Norway.'

There was no response. She was asleep. He stroked her hair and tried to imagine what it would be like being married to her. Her face would be the last thing he saw at night, the first thing he saw in morning. The hours at sea would be spent knowing she was here. And children . . .

It all seemed a little unreal.

Her radio-pager chirped its cheerful tune, and Lara came to with a groan.

'I'll throw that damn thing in the sea!' Magnus vowed, and Lara smiled.

'They'd soon get me a replacement.'

'Lara, you can't go out again. Can't you ring George?'

'Of course not,' she said, already at the telephone. 'It's George's turn tomorrow night — tonight.'

As she listened, her smile died. Her gaze flew to his and the alarm in her eyes had him on his feet and by her side in an instant.

His first thought was Anders, and he prayed that he was wrong. Not now. Not yet . . .

She put out a hand, but when he grasped

it, he had the feeling she was offering reassurance, not seeking it.

'What's wrong?' he asked as she replaced the receiver. 'Is it Anders?'

'No — no, it's not Anders. But I have to go.' She gave his hand another squeeze. 'You'd better come with me, Magnus. It's your mother.'

11

'What are you two doing here?' Shona demanded.

It was with immense relief that Lara saw she was sitting upright in an armchair. On hearing that Shona had collapsed, she hadn't known what she and Magnus might find. Magnus looked terribly shaken, but she could sense his own relief.

'I'm on call,' Lara explained. 'When they bleeped me I was at Braeside with Magnus.'

This information did nothing to improve Shona's already ragged temper. She looked at the two of them, gave the clock a meaningful glance, and pointedly refrained from asking what Lara had been doing at Braeside at such an early hour.

'What happened?' Lara asked calmly.

'I fainted,' Shona declared huffily. 'Dear me, it comes to something when a person can't even — ' She nodded in the direction of a very pale Alisdair. '*He* panicked. I'm perfectly all right.'

Lara couldn't imagine Alisdair panicking for no reason.

'What happened, Ally?'

'She clutched at her side, bent double in agony, and then she just collapsed.' Alisdair shot a glance at his mother. 'She does look better now, but if you'd seen her — '

'Has this happened before?' Lara asked.

'I've had a bit of a pain before, but it soon passes.' Shona said.

'Where's the pain?' Shona pointed to her upper abdomen.

'When you say you've had this pain before — how long has it been going on?'

'A few months,' Shona admitted, 'but it's nothing. It comes and goes. I can go days, weeks even, without any trouble at all.'

Shona's pulse was racing. Having described it as 'nothing', she was clearly getting in a state about it.

'Can I have a cup of tea?' the patient asked testily.

'A drink of water, if you like.'

Alisdair fetched the water before Shona had chance to argue.

'Has the pain ever gone to your shoulder?' Lara asked.

Shona's eyes were brimming with surprise and suspicion. 'Once or twice.'

'Any nausea?' Lara asked.

'A little.'

'Oh, Shona.' Lara patted the shaking hand. 'Why didn't you tell me?'

'Because there are things I'd rather not know about,' Shona declared. 'If I thought I had — what Anders has, I'd rather not know. I hate hospitals. I hate the smell. I hate being poked and prodded. I hate the way doctors hum and ha without saying a thing. In fact, I hate doctors full stop!'

She glared at Lara, who glanced at Magnus and suddenly laughed.

'That's a pity,' she told Shona, 'because you're about to have a doctor for a daughter-in-law.'

Shona's head flew up. She looked at Magnus, who was receiving a painfully hearty slap on the back from Alisdair, and then she looked back at Lara.

'You're going to marry Magnus?' she whispered.

'Yes.' Lara held out her left hand, and Shona's eyes filled with tears.

'Oh, Shona.' Lara said urgently, 'I know I'm not the sort of wife you wanted for Magnus. I can't cook, I can't knit, I can't sew, I hate the sea — but I love him more than I can tell you, and I know I can make him happy.'

Shona, incapable of speech, hugged Lara tight. It was several moments before she accepted the hankie Magnus handed her, and beamed at them both.

'You make him happy already,' she said, and there was joy in her voice. 'It was never you, lass,' she added gently. 'I was against it, I'll admit, but never because of you. Who cares if you can cook? You can learn or you can eat out.

'No, it was Magnus I was worried about. I knew that when he gave his heart, he'd give it completely. I could see nothing but heartbreak for him.'

She reached out a hand to her son. Magnus grasped it, and bent over and kissed her. Shona gazed into his face with so much love in her eyes that the lines of worry around them seemed to melt away.

'Your dad would be so happy and so proud.' Then, before the emotion overwhelmed her completely, she added in that same shaky voice, 'We should be opening champagne.'

'Ha!' Lara scoffed. 'No champagne for you. I want you in bed — now. Can you manage to walk?' she asked, offering a hand.

'Walk?' Shona chuckled. 'I could run, lass. What a tonic!'

For all that, Shona was very unsteady on her feet and Lara gave her a helping hand.

Shona paused, turning to Magnus.

'Don't forget those creels, love.'

'Bed!' Lara urged her on. 'I have to do a

surgery, Shona, and while I'm there, I'll arrange some tests at the hospital. And don't look like that — you'll have to drink a tasteless, harmless chemical and have your picture taken, that's all. A blood test, too.'

Shona shuddered.

'Shona, it's more likely to be gallstones than anything.'

Shona expelled her breath on a shaky sigh of relief.

'As you're such a baby,' Lara teased, 'I'll go to the hospital with you.'

'Lara — thank you,' Shona whispered.

'Don't mention it. I do it for all my difficult patients.'

'I didn't mean that.' Shona chuckled.

Realisation dawned. Lara grinned, and bent to kiss her. 'You're thanking me for marrying the man I love?'

'I don't expect it was an easy decision.'

'I don't think the decision was ever mine to make.'

Shona understood. 'I was just the same with his dad . . . '

Lara squeezed her hand.

'Now, you rest until I get back. I'll leave you some painkillers. Hopefully you won't need them, but just in case . . . '

Magnus and Alisdair were in the kitchen, looking very serious, and very close.

'She's going to be all right,' Lara promised them.

They both made noises intended to show Lara that they hadn't doubted it for a moment, but their faces showed their anxiety.

'I haven't even kissed my future sister-in-law.' Alisdair's mischievous side showed itself as she was given an enormous bear hug and kissed very thoroughly.

'That's enough, Ally,' Magnus said, exasperated, 'you've made your point!' Laughing, Alisdair released her.

'Magnus has asked me to be best man so I hope you've got some beautiful bridesmaids for me to take care of.'

'I haven't had chance to think about it.' Lara said. 'Fran, of course. And I wonder if Rachel — Yes, she'd love it!'

'She certainly would.' Alisdair smiled.

'I'll have a word with Anna.' She smiled at Magnus. 'We'll have to see the minister, too. If ever we get a minute . . .

'I'll have to go.' She looked to them both. 'Will you stay with Shona?'

'I will,' Alisdair replied, and Lara nodded her satisfaction.

'If she's in any pain, ring me. OK?'

'Of course.' Alisdair's expression changed. 'Will Anders be at the wedding?'

Lara looked at him as Magnus's arm came

round her shoulders.

'I hope so. Even if he can't make it to the service, at least he'll be able to see us in all our finery.'

'Finery?' Magnus asked warily.

'Finery!' Lara poked him in the ribs. 'I must dash. After surgery, I'll take Shona to hospital. Then we need to see Anders . . . '

'I have to take a look at the *Ermingerd*.' Magnus said, 'and see if those rocks did any damage.'

'We've got divers doing that!' Alisdair shook his head. 'Talk about having a dog and barking yourself.'

Magnus ignored him. 'I'll catch up with you later, Lara, perhaps when you see Anders.'

'Don't forget the creels, Magnus.' Alisdair grinned.

Magnus rolled his eyes to the heavens. 'Chance would be a fine thing!'

'Creels?' Lara asked curiously.

'Mum promised Carol that I'd let her have the creels — you know that old building that belonged to your great-grandfather?'

'You said there was nothing in it.'

'There isn't, except some old useless creels. We were going to throw them out when I moved to Braeside but we never got around to it. The building is part boarded at the roof and Sam — I assume it was Sam — kept all his creels there. The wood was rotten, and the creels were useless so we left well alone.

'However,' he added, 'Carol wants them for her craft shop. She's planning to decorate the walls with old creels and fishing nets.'

'That will look lovely!' Lara exclaimed.

Magnus and Alisdair shared a telling glance.

'Aye, so would wallpaper.' Alisdair grinned. 'I'll bring the ladder over, Magnus, and give you a hand. I'd hate to see you break your neck before the wedding . . .'

★ ★ ★

Lara stopped her car outside Anders' house and waved. He was sitting gazing out of the window. Seeing her, his face lit up and he quickly folded the newspaper and put it aside.

'You've just missed Magnus,' he told her as she bent to kiss him. 'He'd been checking over the *Ermingerd*, but there was no damage that they could — '

His voice stopped abruptly as he saw the circle of diamonds guarding the ruby on Lara's hand.

Lara perched on the edge of his chair and put out her hand for his inspection. As she hugged him gently, those frail arms held her close.

When he released her, he took her left hand in his and gazed in wonder at the ring that had once belonged to his mother; the ring that should have belonged to his wife.

'Magnus never said a word!' He smiled, his voice heavy with emotion. 'I gathered from the silly grin on his face that things were OK, but . . .'

He fell silent, content to hold Lara's hand and watch the sunlight catch the ruby.

'I can't tell you what this would have meant to your grandmother,' he said at last. 'This ring — ' He touched the glowing stone. 'She said that in her dreams she was always wearing it. And sometimes, she dreamed that she'd lost it. She told me of frantic dreams, nightmares she called them, when she searched high and low for this ring. Then, just when it was within reach, she woke up.'

Lara leaned her head on his shoulder.

'But it's not just the ring. That's only metal and stones.'

'Hardly,' Lara argued softly.

'Perhaps you're right. I remember my mother *did* lose it once. Jakob and I, along with most of the neighbours and their children, spent a whole day searching a hillside where she was sure she must have lost it. The ring was so precious to her and she was beside herself. That evening, after giving us instructions to regroup and continue the search at first light, she found it lying beside her sewing basket. She'd been working with some delicate fabric and had removed her ring in case she damaged the material . . .

'But if Moira could only know that you were with Magnus!' His eyes misted. 'She loved him so much. She loved both those boys as if they were her own. And I don't believe she ever had a favourite.

'Alisdair was the same age as you and, through him, you became more real to her. And of course, that impish sense of humour completely stole her heart.

'But Magnus — she loved him for what he was.'

At the laboured sound of his breathing, Lara put a gentle hand against his face. 'Don't tire yourself, Granddad.'

He smiled at her. They both knew there was so much to say, and so little time in which to say it.

'I was a wealthy man, you know, Lara. I still am. When you had land that the oil companies wanted — ' He shrugged. 'There was so much I could have done for Moira. So much I could have given her. But no. She would take nothing. In all the years I knew her — loved her — there was only one occasion when she came to me for help.'

He paused to catch his breath.

'I was at home in Norway, when she telephoned me out of the blue one evening, a couple of months after Robbie died.

'Even now, I can hear the fear in her voice. 'I'm frightened for Magnus,' she said simply. 'I honestly don't think he can cope. He needs a man, Anders. Will you come?' '

'Did you come?' Lara asked softly.

Anders' eyebrows shot up at that.

'Of course!' He smiled. 'The one and only time that Moira asked for my help, it was for Magnus.'

Thoughtfully, he added, 'I'm not sure if my being here helped at all. I like to think it did. But that's all over. Magnus did cope. He came through it with a strength of character second to none, and at peace with himself, too. In someone so young, that's rare.'

'Hush,' Lara said gently. 'Don't talk any more.'

Anders sat quietly for a few minutes until, gradually, his breathing became slightly easier. Then he looked at Lara.

'There is no man on this earth,' he said softly, 'that I would rather leave you with . . . '

* * *

Back home, Lara was a little apprehensive as she tapped out her parent's number.

She was relieved when her father answered, and his reaction, so typical, filled her with longing for him.

'Darling, that's wonderful!' His voice boomed out as if he had to shout from London to Shetland without the aid of a phone. 'I wish you were here, so that I could give my darling girl a hug. Where's the lucky man? Is he with you?'

'No, not at the moment. It's all been a bit hectic.'

'I'll speak to him later then.' her dad told her. 'I'm thrilled, darling, really thrilled. I could see he was in love with you.' He chuckled. 'I should imagine the whole world could see it. But I thought you had doubts — Oh, darling, I'm thrilled.'

'So you said.' Lara laughed.

The laugh caught in her throat. Worrying about Magnus, the lack of sleep, the panic over Shona, the knowledge that she was going to spend the rest of her days with Magnus . . .

'Oh, Dad,' she whispered, 'I am so happy.'

The booming voice was instantly gentle. 'I know, darling. Treasure it.'

'I will,' she promised.

'Married. My little girl getting married!'

Lara heard Margaret's 'Married?' in the background. The joy in her mother's voice filled Lara with relief.

She only caught snippets of the muffled conversation that followed but as she heard the words 'Tony's parents' her spirits fell. Margaret thought she was marrying Tony. Oh, surely not!

'Hang on a minute, darling,' Robert said, 'your mother wants a word . . . '

There were more muffled words that Lara didn't catch. She could picture her father's large hand over the receiver.

Finally Margaret came on the telephone.

'Lara — ' A long silence followed before Margaret said abruptly, 'Your father tells me that you're going to marry — Magnus.'

'That's right.' Lara's voice was sharp, defensive.

'Why? When? For heaven's sake, Lara, have you taken leave of your senses?'

'I love him,' Lara said simply.

Margaret groaned.

'I've got nothing against him but — '

'You've got everything against him,' Lara cried. 'He was born here, so that's his first fault. He's tied up with your past, with your family, and you don't like that, either.'

'Nonsense,' Margaret scoffed, not very convincingly. 'It's just that the two of you

— you hardly know each other. You have nothing in common.'

'I love him,' Lara said again. 'And we're getting married as soon as possible.'

'Why the rush?' Margaret demanded urgently. 'Look, I know how you feel and I can understand it but there's no need to rush. Just wait a while, darling. See how you feel in a year or so. Surely you can do that.'

'Like you and Dad did?' Lara retorted.

'That was different!'

'No, it was exactly the same. You'd only known each other a short time, and you had nothing in common. Dad was the ambitious boy from the city, and you were the girl from the island. There was never any suggestion of you waiting.'

'But that was different,' Margaret cried.

'In what way?'

'It just was!'

A heavy silence descended.

'Oh, Mum. You will come up for the wedding, won't you?'

'Well, yes, but — '

Lara heard her dad's voice, muffled by a hand over the phone, and then her mother's voice was back, completely different in tone.

'Lara, I'll fly up tomorrow morning. Could you meet the plane? The same one we used last time.'

'What? But — ' Lara's horror gave way to a sudden desire to laugh. 'OK. Yes, that will be nice. There will be lots to do — invitations, flowers, dress, photographer — That's a lovely idea, Mum.'

She was still smiling as she replaced the receiver, and she'd gone less than two steps from it, when it rang.

It was her cousin, Fran. Lara settled herself for a long chat.

'How's everything with you?' she asked.

'Terrible!' Fran complained. 'I was supposed to be at an auction today. I went to the viewing yesterday and it was crammed with things I wanted. And today — would you believe it? — my car wouldn't start so I missed it. I could have got there later but all the bits I wanted were due to be sold early.

'Added to that, I've got a dental appointment first thing in the morning. He's a new chap and he doesn't say a word. In fact, he seems more nervous than I am.'

'He probably hasn't had much experience.' Lara grinned. 'I expect he has to concentrate on putting the needle in the right place, and not letting the drill slip.'

'Thanks for those comforting words.' Fran's humour got the better of her.

'Any more moans while you're in the mood?' Lara teased.

'None that spring to mind.' Fran laughed. 'What about you? Do you have any news to cheer me up?'

'Yes, I have actually. I'm getting married . . . '

* * *

Lara's heart was light as she drove to Braeside.

There was no sign of Magnus at the house so she walked down to the old building where her great-grandfather had built his boat. She'd never taken much notice of it before. It was almost on the beach, hidden from view by the bank. The slate roof looked none too safe, she noticed.

The large wooden doors were propped open with stones, and Lara stepped inside. It felt damp and cold, and was lit only by a single lamp that had been rigged up. Nearby was a neat stack of creels.

'Magnus?'

'Don't come up!' he called back.

She looked at the almost vertical ladder that had been tied to the wall.

'I had no intention of coming up,' she said as he appeared at the top of the ladder.

He came down the ladder with ease, carrying an old wooden crate which he

288

dropped on the floor.

'You're filthy!'

He laughed, wiping his hands on black jeans that had started the day a faded shade of blue.

'I know.' He put his hands behind his back, craned forward and kissed the tip of her nose.

'Mum seems to have found a new lease of life,' he told her. 'Thank heavens it's something so easily put right.'

'We tried to break it to her as gently as we could that she would need an operation, but her first concern was whether she would have it before the wedding or after. As I drove her home, she was busy planning her wedding outfit.'

'She said it was a simple operation,' he said.

'It is, darling. I promise. Totally routine. I only wish she'd come to me sooner. I knew she was worrying, yes, but — ' She shook her head. 'If only I'd known she was worrying that she had some terrifying disease.'

'None of us can read minds.'

'No, and she's feeling better already. She'll have the operation on Tuesday, and then she'll need to take it easy for ten days or so. But she'll be fine. Magnus. Really.'

Ignoring the grime, she hugged him.

'Which would you like first, the good

news or the bad news?'

'Give me the good,' he said warily.

'I rang my parents. Dad was delighted and he says he'll speak to you later.'

'Really?' He was surprised, and pleased.

'I spoke to Fran, too.' She chuckled. 'She's decided on green velvet for the bridesmaids' dresses.'

His face fell.

'So the bad news is your mother?'

Lara nodded.

'How bad is bad?'

'All being well, she'll be on the next plane.'

'What? Tomorrow? You're joking, aren't you? Please tell me you're joking. Marvellous,' he muttered, 'first you can't get the woman within a hundred miles of the place and now you can't keep her away.

'Right,' he added with grim determination. 'we'll see John this evening and get a date fixed. She can't go against the minister, can she?' His scowl relaxed a little. 'Is that all right with you?'

'Fine.' Lara couldn't help her laughter.

'And we'll settle on the first date he can manage?'

'Of course,' Lara promised.

Magnus was satisfied, although Lara did catch something that sounded like 'confounded woman.'

'She'll come round, Magnus,' she said quietly.

'And if she doesn't?'

'She will,' Lara said confidently, 'especially if we mention grandchildren at regular intervals.'

His expression remained doubtful.

'Magnus, will you stop worrying! Mum couldn't make me change my mind about a hideous pair of red shoes I once wanted so she certainly won't be able to change my mind about you. I didn't inherit Anders' stubbornness for nothing, you know.'

He smiled at that.

Lara pointed to the timber above them. 'How's it going?'

'Almost finished. Ally's gone to get some fish and chips. We've been here for hours, and he realised we hadn't eaten.' He nodded to the creels. 'That's the lot but there's a load of old junk up there. I don't know what it is with your family. Moira hoarded anything and everything, and her father — you wouldn't believe what Sam kept!

'We thought that whilst we were at it we'd clear it all out and get rid of all that rotten timber. Some of the kids play around here in the summer and I wouldn't like them to go climbing up there.'

Lara shivered.

'This stuff's been here for fifty years or more,' Magnus said, looking at various boxes and sacks. 'Somewhere — ' he pointed, 'over there is an old newspaper dated 1940.'

'Really?'

Fascinated, Lara picked up the newspaper, carried it closer to the light, brushed the worst of the dust off a box and sat down. The paper was damp and had yellowed with age, and as she unfolded it, it began to disintegrate.

'Look,' she said sadly, 'here's the story of the Coventry air raid. So many people killed. Poor Sam. It seems so unfair to lose his wife like that. Coventry was nothing to her. She was only visiting.'

Magnus nodded. 'It was a terrible time for everyone.'

'We ought to keep this,' Lara said, 'as a souvenir.'

'Why on earth would he want an old, damp newspaper as a souvenir?' His laughter held a note of despair. 'Lara, I'm trying to get rid of your family's souvenirs.'

'I suppose so. It's a strange story though, don't you think? Just think about Sam. He lost his wife, and with her, all interest in life. But he did live, just long enough to save the lives of Anders and the rest of the men on that boat. And then, to die on that very night.'

A shiver ran the length of her spine.

'It was lucky for Anders that he didn't die sooner.' Magnus smiled indulgently. 'But they'd limped back from Norway and I expect, without Sam's help, they would have limped on a bit further until another boat spotted them.'

'You're so practical!'

'One of us has to be.' Magnus laughed. 'Any more souvenirs you'd like before we have the big bonfire? An old sack, perhaps? A box of rusty nails?'

'No, thank you.' She giggled.

'You're quite sure? A nice sack like this? We could hang it on the wall, have it framed perhaps.'

As he lifted the sack it hit the side of the box with a thud.

'There's something in it.' He grinned. 'Probably the skeleton of a long-deceased rat.'

'Magnus!'

'It's probably — ' He opened the sack and peered inside. 'Jesus!' His voice altered.

'What is it?' Lara asked, her voice filled with dread. Beneath the dust and dirt, his face had gone frighteningly pale.

'Magnus? What is it? Is it something — dead?'

Slowly he reached to the bottom of the sack and when Lara saw what he pulled out, her hand flew to her mouth.

She looked at Magnus but she couldn't utter a word.

'This is — ' He held the battered object in his hands as if it were more sacred than life itself.

Lara knew exactly what it was. She'd recognised it immediately from the photograph Anders had shown her. She'd thought then how very small and insignificant it looked, and she thought the same thing now. For all that, she couldn't resist touching it.

She couldn't resist touching Magnus, either. She clutched at his arm, clinging to the living, breathing, comforting solidness of him.

Disconnected images flashed through her mind. Tony applying for the post in Shetland; the vacancy that she'd thought at the time had been sent by Lady Luck: the way her life had become entwined with Magnus's: the way she had found her grandfather just in time. And now this . . .

'How's this for a souvenir?' Magnus kissed the top of her head.

Lara couldn't answer. Her heart was full of Jakob, her great-uncle, little more than a boy at the time, who had put the safekeeping of this insignificant piece of metal before his own safety. And of Sam, her great-grandfather, who must have taken it off that damaged boat to safety, only to die so soon after the task had been completed. And of Anders, her beloved grandfather, who was after all to be granted his wish.

'The Kristiansund Jewel,' Magnus said in amazement. His smile was jubilant, triumphant. 'The Kristiansund Jewel!'

12

Lara sat on the edge of Anders' bed while Magnus pulled up a chair.

The previous evening had taken its toll on Anders, emotionally even more than physically.

Last night, two weeks after they'd found the Kristiansund Jewel, the grateful Norwegians had laid on a 'small' reception in Anders' honour.

Long speeches had been followed by several presentations, and Anders was surrounded by letters of gratitude from the Norwegian people. There was an engraved miniature of the Kristiansund Jewel, a glass bowl with a superb engraving of the Kristiansund Jewel on it . . .

'Too much wine, women and song for you last night,' Lara scolded softly.

'You could be right.' His smile was rueful.

Margaret had attended the reception, and even she had been moved by her father's speech of thanks in which he'd paid tribute to the men who'd given their lives during the war so that the generations that followed could live in peace.

Lara would never forget those strong Norwegian voices proudly singing '*Ja, vi elsker dette landet . . .* ' Neither would she forget the pride in Anders' eyes as he had silently mouthed the words of Norway's national anthem while those powerful voices filled the hall.

'It was a wonderful evening though,' Lara said.

'It was,' Anders agreed, 'but I felt such a fraud.'

'A fraud?' Magnus was amazed.

'Yes, I did nothing. Jakob saved the Jewel from enemy hands, not me. It should have been Jakob standing there last night.'

'Jakob's memory is being honoured, too,' Lara pointed out gently. 'They're dedicating a plaque to his memory, and everyone who visits the museum and sees the Kristiansund Jewel will see the name of Jakob Larsen.'

Anders gestured to the many mementoes of the previous evening. 'But what's the point of all this? Fancy giving these things to a dying man. It's such a waste.'

'It is not!' Lara cried.

'But when I'm gone — What use will it be? It won't mean anything to anyone.'

'Of course it will,' Magnus said gently.

'It certainly will.' Lara squeezed her grandfather's hand. 'It will mean a lot to me and Magnus, our children, and their children. When we tell our children how proud we are of their great-grandfather, we'll be able to show them that the whole of Norway is proud of him, too.'

His eyes were closed as he lay back against a mountain of white pillows and yet his gentle smile told of thoughts that were a world away. Perhaps he could picture those children . . .

'Tell them about Jakob, too.'

Lara held his frail hand to her face.

'We'll tell them about Jakob, about Moira, about Sam — we'll tell them the whole story.'

★ ★ ★

Moira's pride and joy, her airy, sun-blessed conservatory, looked as if a tornado had passed through it. Boxes, books, photographs, and ornaments were scattered everywhere.

Lara and her mother had decided to clear out Moira's things but when Magnus arrived, there was little progress visible.

Lara was taking a photograph of people that even Margaret didn't recognise from a frame and replacing it with a photograph of Robbie, Shona, Magnus and Alisdair.

'I'll see if your mum wants this, Magnus, but if not, I thought we'd put it in the sitting room.'

'Fine, but where's this mountain of stuff to be thrown out?'

'That's the pile that I want to see Shona about.' Lara pointed. 'Mum's taking that lot. We're keeping this.' She pointed again, to a large pile in the corner. 'And somewhere — yes, there, that's the stuff we're throwing out.'

Magnus inspected the things to be thrown out. 'Two photos, two letters and a 1924 cookery book.' He laughed. 'So we're not actually throwing anything away, we're just spreading it around a bit.'

'We've still got a lot to do,' Lara protested.

'Isn't it strange, Lara?' Margaret stopped what she was doing. 'To think that I was born in this house, and in three days time, it will be your home.' Her expression changed. 'I hope you'll be happier than I was.'

'Don't be silly, Mum. Of course I shall!'

Magnus wrapped his arms around Lara's waist. 'I shall beat her mercilessly if she isn't.'

Lara smiled as her mother laughed. Her mother had come to Shetland with the sole intention of showing Lara just how disastrous marriage to Magnus would be, but now she could see that the love they shared was real and lasting.

It was Magnus's relentless teasing that had softened Margaret's heart. That, and the tenderness with which he'd cared for Anders on his 'glory day'.

'Here's my Bible!' Margaret exclaimed suddenly. 'Look, it even has photos of the Holy Land as it is now — or perhaps I should say as it was when I was given this.' She closed the book and ran her hands over the soft blue cover. 'Anders gave me this. Every adult I knew had their very own copy and, of course, I wanted one, too.

'I'd never seen anything like this one,' she added with a smile. 'All the others I'd seen were very dull. They had black covers, small print and certainly no photographs. I thought this was the most marvellous thing I'd ever seen. The sort of Bible that royalty must own.' Her expression clouded. 'Not that I ever told Anders that, of course.'

'You know where he is,' Magnus pointed out quietly.

'Mmm.' Margaret looked up at him. 'You don't have a very high opinion of me, do you, Magnus?'

The question took Lara completely by surprise. She held her breath. Magnus wouldn't lie to spare anyone's feelings.

'I understand,' he replied at last, 'how things that happen during our childhood can scar us for life if we let them.'

'Your father,' Margaret murmured, 'but his

drowning didn't scar you, did it?'

'It changed me. For a long, long time I was very angry, very bitter. And children can be far more bitter and angry than adults if the need arises. I suspect it's all too easy to carry that bitterness into adulthood.'

Margaret nodded.

'And I had it a lot easier than you,' Magnus went on. 'I had a mother, and a brother. Anders, Moira, the whole community behind me. You had no one.

'My father was dead, and I had to accept that. But what happened to you — it was never over, was it? It was an on-going thing. It was always there to feed the bitterness.'

Margaret placed her hand on his arm.

'Yes,' she said. There were tears in her eyes. 'You do understand.'

Magnus took a deep breath, Lara was amused to see, before he hugged her.

Margaret drew away first, and smiled at him shakily.

'May I have this?' She gestured to the Bible.

'Of course.' Magnus was surprised. 'It's yours.'

Margaret ran a gentle hand over the cover and then put it aside. She found more photographs that had been taken on her wedding day.

'That reminds me,' she said. 'A honey-moon.'

'Mum,' Lara protested, 'we've been over this.'

'So it won't hurt to go over it again,' Margaret replied firmly. 'A honeymoon is important, it really is. I can remember every moment of mine, and I'll treasure those memories for ever. Granted, a lot of newly-weds can't afford a honeymoon and if that's the case, there's nothing that can be done about it. But I still say it's important.

'Marriage is hard. Yes, I know,' she went on as Lara was about to argue, 'I'm not so blind that I can't recognise a couple in love when I see one. And I have no doubt that your marriage will work. But for all that, it will be hard at times.'

'We know that, Mum,' Lara said carefully, 'and we *are* having a honeymoon. We're going to Norway. But not yet.'

Her mother looked straight at her.

'You're intending to wait for Anders to die! You're so wrong, Lara. You'll tell yourselves that he had a good life, that you wouldn't have wanted him to suffer any longer, but his death will still come as a shock, affect you both deeply.' She threw up her hands in despair. 'It'll be more of a wake than a honeymoon!'

Lara felt Magnus' arms tighten around her.

'Have a honeymoon,' Margaret pleaded. 'Go to Norway now, while Anders is still able to share in it with you. Bring him back photos of his beloved Norway, of the Kristiansund Jewel, the plaque they've put up in Jakob's memory . . .'

Lara turned to look at Magnus. She could see her own feelings mirrored in his eyes.

If only they could tell Anders they'd seen the Kristiansund Jewel in the land where it belonged, show him a photograph of Jakob's plaque, describe it all to him . . .

But life wasn't that simple.

'We can't, Mum, it's out of the question. You know how ill he is, and how quickly he's deteriorating. He needs — well, what he needs is constant nursing but, of course, he won't hear of that.

'Shona's making a good recovery, true, but she couldn't take on anything like that. No, it's out of the question.

'The one good thing about Magnus' work is that when he's home, he can spend time with Anders. With my job, I can't do that.

'And we're not the best people. Anders likes to talk to us and we can't hear enough of his story. Instead of doing things for him, we tend to spend all our time sitting talking to him.'

Margaret walked over to the window and gazed out for a few moments. Then she turned to face them.

'I'll take care of him.'

Lara gasped. She looked at Magnus, but all she saw there was a reflection of her own shock.

'Why not?' Margaret demanded. 'I can stay for as long as it takes. Rob will manage.

'I can even move in with Anders . . . he's got plenty of room. Let's face it, he's not in a position to argue, is he?'

'Would you do that?' Magnus asked.

Tears sprang to Margaret's eyes. 'He *is* my father, you know!'

With a choked cry, Lara rushed forward and hugged her mother tight. They held each other for several minutes.

'I never thought I'd live long enough to hear you say that, Mum.'

'I never thought I'd be able to say it,' Margaret admitted. 'Or that I'd want to say it.'

When Lara released her, Margaret fumbled for a hankie.

'Magnus, will you please take my daughter on a honeymoon?'

'The pleasure will be all mine!' Magnus promised.

★ ★ ★

The day dawned dull, damp and misty but the mist was slowly clearing and even the wind had dropped. It wasn't the perfect day for a wedding but at least the guests weren't likely to get drenched or blown off their feet. Waiting for the car, Lara couldn't believe how quiet the house was after all the pandemonium.

'Feeling nervous?' her dad asked gently.

'No.' Lara smiled. 'What is there to be nervous about? This dress — ' She touched the white satin and laughed softly. 'Magnus would think I looked terrific if I turned up in an old pair of jeans and a sack!

'And I don't need to worry about him being at the kirk. If he's not there, I'll know he's rescuing stricken fishing boats or stranded whales!'

Robert laughed.

'All the whales in the world wouldn't keep Magnus away. I wonder if he's feeling nervous. I know I was on my wedding day.'

Lara didn't know. She'd spoken to Shona earlier and she'd sounded anything but calm. Even Alisdair, coming to the phone to give Lara his best wishes, had sounded unusually tense.

But she didn't know if Magnus would be

feeling nervous or not. She did know that he had no need to be. Any number of things could go wrong but at the end of the day, their love would have been blessed in front of God. What else mattered?

'Ah, here's the car.' Remembering Margaret's dire threats about crumpling the yards of white satin, he hugged Lara with great care. 'This is where I'm supposed to say something profound, darling, and I can't think of a single thing.'

'There's nothing to say, Dad. It's all been said.' Tears of happiness shone in Lara's eyes

'Yes, it has. When you think of Anders and Margaret, not knowing each other, not getting on with each other — We've had it all, Lara. We've been so lucky.'

'We still have it, Dad.' Lara held him close.

'And always shall.' He took her hand. 'Let's go, darling . . . '

★ ★ ★

An excited murmur and a sudden shuffling alerted Magnus to Lara's arrival at the kirk. He checked his watch. She was four minutes late.

Alisdair, next to him, turned his head to see but Magnus was suddenly distracted.

More than twenty years ago, standing in

this kirk, at his father's funeral, Magnus had been chilled by the very blackness of the day. Then Moira, standing close to him, had murmured in his ear.

'The sun will shine for you again, Magnus. The calm always follows the storm, the morning always follows the night and the spring always follows the winter . . .'

He could hear her voice . . .

Now, as if it were Moira's wedding gift, the sun was shining. In fact, in the many hundreds of times that Magnus had been in this kirk since, he had never seen anything like it.

The sun had been pale and weak all morning, but now its beams were like powerful searchlights. Shafts of sunlight danced on the walls, and on the flowers. Each flower took its turn under the brilliant spotlight . . .

'Oh!'

Alisdair's soft exclamation brought Magnus from his daydreams. He turned to look, past the guests in their bright colours, to a dazzling vision of white — brilliant white.

The sun focused completely on Lara. It teased her hair, making it gleam like silver. It touched her eyes, deepening the blue and highlighting the silver-grey flecks. It lit her smile.

She would never know how beautiful she looked at that moment . . .

★ ★ ★

Lara hadn't imagined the celebrations would go on quite so long. The guests looked as if they might dance for ever. Anders had been taken home a long time ago, just after the reception, tired but immensely happy. Shona, still recovering from her operation, had called it a day, too, albeit somewhat reluctantly. Everyone else, though, was going strong.

Her family were trying — unsuccessfully for the most part — to master the traditional dances.

Fran was dancing with Tony, leaning close to make herself heard above the music, and Tony threw back his head and laughed.

That pleased Lara. Tony might know that there could never have been a future for them, but knowing it wouldn't have made today any easier for him.

Lara spotted her patient, Anna Thompson, and made her way over to her.

'How are you feeling?'

Anna laughed.

'Can't you stop being a doctor for five minutes? This is your wedding day!'

'I wasn't being a doctor,' Lara protested. 'I

was asking as a friend.'

'I'm fine. I'll admit that I felt a bit shaky this morning. It was the thought of so many people, having to smile all the time, and knowing that, come what may, I had to cope for Rachel's sake. But it's been a lovely day, Lara.'

Lara gazed at the army of friends and relatives, and at Magnus who was talking to Robert while watching Lara at the same time.

'Perfect.'

'Oh, just look at Rachel,' Anna said with dismay.

Her little daughter, as pretty as any bridesmaid could be, was dragging Alisdair onto the dance floor — again.

'He's loving every moment of it.' Lara laughed. 'He takes one look at Rachel and melts, you know he does. And she's not monopolising him. I stole him for a dance, and he danced with Fran a couple of times. And,' she added, remembering the flush she'd spotted on Anna's cheeks, 'I saw him dancing with you, Anna.'

The flush returned immediately. 'Aye, well — '

'You dance well together.'

'We've danced together before,' Anna told her awkwardly.

'Yes, I know what happened. Ally told me.'

'I'm surprised he remembers.' Anna smiled.

'Oh, he remembers. All six weeks and four days of it.'

Anna was blushing furiously.

'I'd better go and distract Rachel.' Anna went over and took her daughter firmly by the hand.

Alisdair was standing where they'd left him, Lara noticed. His thoughts were clearly miles away, and his gaze was on Anna.

Lara crossed the room to him. Even when she was standing right beside him, he didn't notice her.

'Something on your mind, Ally?'

'What?' Startled, he laughed softly. 'No, not really.'

'I do believe,' Lara teased gently, 'that Anna stole a tiny piece of your heart and never thought to give it back.'

'Now there you're wrong. It wasn't a tiny piece at all.'

'Mmm,' Lara murmured thoughtfully, 'and Anna isn't as immune to you as she'd like the world to believe.'

'No, she isn't, is she?' Alisdair grinned.

They were both watching Anna when she looked in Alisdair's direction — her cheeks scarlet as she became aware of their eyes.

'Within twelve months,' Alisdair vowed softly, 'two years at the most, we'll all be back here for another wedding.'

'And I thought you were already promised to Rachel,' Lara teased.

'I don't think she'd be too unhappy if I married her mother instead.'

'I'm sure she'd be delighted.' Lara chuckled. 'So you've convinced me, and convincing Rachel will be easy — all you have to do now is convince Anna.'

'That might take a while, but you, better than anyone else, ought to know just how fatal the Cameron charm can be. She won't stand a chance . . .'

Laughing, he put his arms round his sister-in-law's waist and waltzed her on to the dance floor.

★ ★ ★

'I don't know why I'm still waving,' Margaret said, 'I can't even see them.'

They soon wouldn't be able to see the boat, Anders thought with amusement, as Margaret fumbled in her handbag. Anders took a crisply folded handkerchief from his pocket and handed it to her. It had been the same in the kirk yesterday.

'Thanks. I don't know why I'm crying, either. Yesterday — today — I can't seem to stop.'

'She was a truly beautiful bride,' Anders said calmly.

'Radiant. And Magnus — did you ever see a man look happier?' Margaret smiled as she mopped her eyes.

'No.'

'Do you remember that day on the beach, when Lara was five and Magnus was ten? Do you remember how reluctant he was to take her along the beach and how appalled he was at the very idea of having to hold her hand?'

'Yes.'

'And do you remember how she screamed when he found that dead bird? How she made us promise that she would never have to see that horrid boy again?'

'I remember.' He remembered, too, Moira's wistful expression as she had watched those children, both so very dear to her heart, set off along the beach together.

'Isn't it strange how life's come full circle?' Margaret slipped her arm through her father's.

'It is,' Anders agreed.

'I've never heard Lara laugh so often. I've never seen her so happy, and it's all down to Magnus.'

'I'm glad you're getting to know Magnus. You've never done him justice, my dear.'

'I know,' Margaret whispered.

'She'll want for nothing,' Anders promised Margaret. 'I don't mean materially. I mean emotionally.'

'Oh, Anders, you can't imagine what a relief it is to see your daughter married to the right person. To know that, whatever the future holds, he'll be with her.'

Anders didn't have to imagine. He knew. He'd known that same relief when Robert had come into Margaret's life. He'd known it would take someone very special to bring real happiness to Margaret . . .

'Anders?' Her voice faltered slightly. 'Do you mind me staying with you?'

He gazed at her, not understanding.

'I know you agreed to it for Magnus and Lara's sake, so they would go to Norway without worrying about you. But do you mind? Really?'

'Will there ever come a day when you're not happy to see Lara?' Anders asked curiously.

'Well, no — of course not.' It was Margaret's turn to be confused.

'My dear Meg,' Anders said softly, 'there will never come a day when I'm not happy to see you, either.'

He felt her hand tighten on his arm, and they both looked out to the speck that was the ferry.

Silently, Anders offered his thanks to God. Thanks for bringing Lara to him, for bringing his daughter back into his life, for giving him enough time to finally put the wrongs right.

And for so much more . . .

Some would say it was an old man's fanciful imagination. Others would say it was the effects of too much medicine. Some might even say it had been those sudden, startling bursts of sunlight playing tricks on his mind.

No one on earth would convince Anders that Moira hadn't been by his side as Magnus and Lara had made their vows before God. Nor would anyone convince him that Moira wasn't with him now.

He could feel her heart — so young, free, and full of loving — warming his own. He could hear her calling to him. He could see her smile welcoming him.

Soon, my love, he promised silently.

Soon, very soon, he would once again walk hand in hand with the woman he loved. Leaning on the ferry's rails, with Magnus' arm around her shoulders, Lara gazed down at the water.

'I must be mad. It was all well and good to compromise — go by boat one way and by plane the other — but why did I let myself be talked into going by boat? I'll probably spend

314

the entire fortnight feeling ill.'

'Nonsense.' Magnus laughed. 'I got a forecast before we left and it's like a duck pond out there.'

'I expect your idea of a duck pond is vastly different to mine.'

Laughing, he hugged her.

'I promise you'll hardly know we're moving. And think how much you'll see, far more than you will from the plane.'

'Sea, more sea and even more sea!' She groaned with laughter.

Lara rested her head on his shoulder, her thoughts drifting back over the last twenty-four hours.

She would never forget how she and her father had instinctively paused as they had entered the crowded kirk. The brilliant sunshine had surprised them both.

The service had passed in a daze, moving into slow motion as they had solemnly exchanged vows. And then the sunlight had danced on those matching gold bands . . .

'Did you like my dress?' She murmured.

'You looked beautiful, darling.' She saw again the wonder in his eyes.

'But my dress — ' Her voice was teasing. 'Describe it to me.'

'Well, it was white.' He gave a short laugh then ran a thoughtful finger across his chin.

'It was long. And if ever I need to refresh my memory, I'm sure we'll be keeping it as a souvenir of the day.' He drew her close.

'You're right, if I were given a choice of only two, I wouldn't recognise your dress. But if I were a blind man, dying in some far-flung land, I would recognise the touch of your hand above all others.'

'As I would yours . . .'

As he kissed her, she wondered again at all those years she had lived without even knowing he existed. The man was more precious to her than life itself.

She thanked God, as she did every day, for bringing her to him — for bringing her home.

The kiss deepened, and in that kiss was a promise. A promise that the real story — their story — was only just beginning.

THE END

We do hope that you have enjoyed reading
this large print book.

Did you know that all of our titles
are available for purchase?

We publish a wide range of high quality
large print books including:
Romances, Mysteries, Classics,
General Fiction,
Non Fiction and Westerns.

Special interest titles available in
large print are:
The Little Oxford Dictionary
Music Book
Song Book
Hymn Book
Service Book

Also available from us courtesy of Oxford
University Press:
Young Readers' Dictionary
(large print edition)
Young Readers' Thesaurus
(large print edition)

For further information or a free
brochure, please contact us at:
Ulverscroft Large Print Books Ltd.,
The Green, Bradgate Road, Anstey,
Leicester, LE7 7FU, England.
Tel: (00 44) 0116 236 4325
Fax: (00 44) 0116 234 0205

NO TIME LIKE THE PRESENT

June Barraclough

Daphne Berridge, who has never married, has retired to the small Yorkshire village of Heckcliff where she grew up, intending to write the biography of an eighteenth-century woman poet. Two younger women are interested in her project: Cressida, Daphne's niece, who lives in London, and is uncertain about the direction of her life; and Judith, who keeps a shop in Heckcliff, and is a divorcee. When an old friend of Daphne falls in love with Judith, the question — as for Cressida — is marriage or independence. Then Daphne also receives a surprise proposal.

SEARCH FOR A SHADOW

Kay Christopher

On the last day of her holiday Rosemary Roberts met an intriguing American in the foyer of her London hotel. By some extraordinary coincidence, Larry Madison-Jones was due to visit the tiny Welsh village where Rosemary lived. But how much of a coincidence was Larry's erratic presence there? The moment Rosemary returned home, her life took on a subtle, though sinister edge — Larry had a secret he was not willing to share. As Rosemary was drawn deeper into a web of mysterious and suspicious occurrences, she found herself wondering if Larry really loved her — or was trying to drive her mad . . .

THREE WISHES

Barbara Delinsky

Slipping and sliding in the snow as she walks home from the restaurant where she's worked for fourteen years, Bree Miller barely has time to notice the out-of-control lorry, headed straight for her. All Bree remembers of that fateful night is a bright light, and a voice granting her three wishes. Are they real or imagined? And who is the man standing over her bedside when finally she wakes up? Soon Bree finds herself the recipient of precisely those things she'd most wanted in life — even that which had seemed beyond all reasonable hope.

WEB OF WAR

Hilary Grenville

Claire Grant, a radar operator in the WAAF, still mourning the death of her parents and brother in an air raid, finds coming on leave to her grandmother's home difficult to face. Martin, a friend from her school days, now a pilot in the RAF, helps her to come to terms with her grief and encourages the flimsy rapport between Claire and her grandmother. War rules their lives and it is some time before they meet again. Claire is in love, but there are many quirks of fate yet to be faced.